MW01147965

Stolen Kisses

The Barrington Billionaires
Book Two

Ruth Cardello

Author Contact
website: RuthCardello.com
email: Minouri@aol.com
Facebook: Author Ruth Cardello
Twitter: RuthieCardello

Dax Marshall isn't the type of man a woman takes home to meet her parents. He's a business shark who has never let anything as insignificant as caring stop him from taking over a company. Some call him heartless, but he doesn't see the value of caring about anyone or anything until he meets Kenzi.

Her happiness becomes his obsession.

Kenzi Barrington has tried to be the person her family needed her to be, but she doesn't want to lie anymore. When she can't hold a dark secret in another day, she turns to the one man she knows is strong enough to hear the truth.

What starts as a simple attraction becomes a friendship that changes how they both define love.

Be the first to hear about my releases
ruthcardello.com/signup

One random newsletter subscriber will be chosen every month in 2015. The chosen subscriber will receive a $100 eGift Card! Sign up today by clicking on the link above!

COPYRIGHT

Dedication

This book is dedicated to survivors and those who stand with them.

A Note to My Readers

There are no easy fixes when it comes to surviving a trauma. There is no magical way to erase the past or guarantee that people will respond well when we need them to. All we can do is stay strong and loving and fill our lives with people who enrich it. As you read Stolen Kisses, I hope you see love through my eyes. Not simply as the romantic love that the story revolves around, but also as the complex relationships we all have with our friends, our family and ourselves. It's said so often that it's easy to dismiss as trite, but: To truly love anyone, you must first love yourself. That's the journey Kenzi and Dax are on.

Chapter One

WITH HER HIGH heels swinging from one hand and a half empty bottle of rum from the other, Kenzi Barrington walked along an empty stretch of her favorite Bahamian island beach. The warm sand was a familiar comfort. Music blared from the nearby hotel pool area, but that wasn't what stopped Kenzi from finding peace that night.

She raised the bottle to her lips and took another long gulp. She sought numbness. Distance. Denial. The fruity drinks the bar served had no kick so she'd bribed the bartender for a bottle of her own and left.

Out of the corner of her eye she saw a man in a dark suit, watching her from a path beside the beach. His face was darkened in shadow, but the breadth of his shoulders and his impressive height left little question about why he was following her: Her family had sent a bodyguard, even though she'd told them she didn't want one. As the youngest of seven, six of whom were unfortunately brothers, she was used to no one respecting her wishes.

How did I ever think they would let me do a reality show?

They've never let me do anything. Disappointment sucker-punched her as she remembered the final conversation she'd had with the Hollywood producer. He'd been interested in the idea she'd pitched, interested enough to draw up the contracts for her to read over. Then, at their last meeting, he'd announced he wasn't moving forward with the project. Suddenly, just like every other opportunity or idea she'd ever had, it had been shut down.

Why did I let myself believe this time would be different? Although being followed around by cameras and letting the world see her day-to-day life should have been scary, Kenzi thought it could free her. *Force me to face what I can no longer deny.*

Does it matter? It's not happening.

When the producer slipped up and said he couldn't meet with her again, Kenzi had instantly been suspicious. *Couldn't? As in, been warned not to?*

Although the producer had denied it, the truth had been there in his cautious eyes. He'd been scared. She'd seen the look before. Her brothers plowed over people, silenced those who opposed them, and crushed scandals before they went public. *Maybe stopping me is for the best, too.*

But my silence should be my choice.

She knew she wasn't making sense anymore, but the alcohol fueled her anger toward her brothers. Kenzi raised the bottle in salute to the bodyguard then dropped her shoes into the sand. After one final swig, she dropped the bottle beside her shoes and glared at the man who hadn't moved. She could feel his eyes on her, and her hands clenched at her sides. Like thoughts of her family, his presence held her back from enjoying the novelty of a strong buzz. Instead of the giddy oblivion she'd sought, she felt raw, cornered. Watched. Always watched, but never heard. She wanted to sink to her knees in the sand and cry. Instead, she called out, "Tell my family you couldn't find me, or say you saw me go into my hotel room. Go away. I want to be alone."

His rigid outline stood in quiet judgment of her, and she hated him for it. Hated feeling like, even here at her island escape, she was being controlled. An impulse to defy him made her turn toward the waves. She would disappear into the darkness and lose herself in her exercise of choice. She shed her dress in one swift move, without embarrassment; her navy-blue bra and panties covered more than many bikinis anyway. She was ankle-deep in the water when a strong hand closed over her arm and hauled her back two steps then swung her around.

"Whatever you're running from, killing yourself isn't the answer," the bodyguard said impatiently, with a hint of an English accent.

Kenzi tried to yank her arm free, but he held her easily. She turned angry eyes toward his face, and her next words died on her lips. He was an attractive man but not in a male-model way. His features were harsh; his nose was slightly crooked as if it had been broken once or twice. He wasn't at all what Kenzi would have said was her taste. The men she dated took as long styling their hair as she did. This was a *man*. Her heart beat wildly in her chest. Nothing about his expression hinted he might be attracted to her, yet her stomach quivered with excitement. She dismissed the temporary insanity of her libido as a result of too much rum. She hoped she sounded angry instead of breathless when she said, "I am an excellent swimmer. And I don't appreciate being manhandled." Even to her own ears, her voice sounded slurred.

He dropped his hand from her arm. "You're drunk, and I don't have time for the police investigation that will follow your body being washed up on the shore tomorrow morning." He gave her a slow once-over then bent to pick up her dress. He threw it at her. "Get dressed. I'm walking you back to the hotel."

Kenzi clenched her dress in front her. "No." It was hard to deny her level of inebriation as she swayed. Okay, so swimming might have been a bad idea, but did he have to speak to her like she was a child?

A hint of a smile stretched one side of his amazing lips. "Don't test me on this."

It was surprisingly exciting to defy him, and that feeling was preferable to the many dark emotions swirling through her. She let herself imagine how his mouth would feel on hers and licked her bottom lip as she stared at his. "I'm not testing you. I'm telling you I'm not going anywhere with you. I don't care who hired you or how much they're paying you. I don't need you." *Well, not in any way I can say.* Would a night in his arms achieve what neither the beach nor the rum had? Would it free her, if only for a short time? *Stupid. Stupid idea.* One-night stands hadn't helped her feel better in the past, adding another to her list wouldn't now. *Maybe this is exactly what I deserve. No. Stop thinking like that. I am not the person I almost became.* "Please, go find someone else to protect."

She backed up a step and turned away, but tripped over her shoes and face-planted in the sand. She raised herself onto her hands and spat out the sand that had flown into her mouth.

He hauled her back to her feet. "Are you—?"

In her impaired state, that's all it took for an old memory, one she'd tried so many times to wipe away, to blur the present with the past. He was no longer the alluring bodyguard ruining her attempt to find peace. There was no longer anything sexy about teasing him. He was another man in another time, who was holding her, and she couldn't get away. Shame. Rage. Adrenaline rushed in as it had so many times she'd tried to be intimate with a man. Alcohol wasn't as effective at numbing her as the drugs she'd used in the past. It only gave more life to her panic when it came. When she struggled to free herself, he clamped another hand on her other arm, and she lost all control. She started to flail wildly, kicking at him with desperation. "Don't touch me!" she cried out, but her warning was garbled as the rum took full effect.

He held her against him and said, "What the bloody hell is wrong with you? I'm not going to hurt you. I'm trying to help."

It might have been the authoritative tone he used, or maybe the way he was calm despite her hysteria, that brought her back to the present. The shame she'd spent half her life running from followed. She shook her head back and forth, and his face blurred behind tears she only let herself shed here on this island or on stage when the emotion could be passed off as someone else's. "Just leave me alone. Walk away."

"Trust me, if I could, I would." His voice was harsh, but his hold on her gentled. He was still holding her against him, but suddenly it was different. There was protectiveness in his embrace that hadn't been there a moment before. "Who are you?"

Her eyes flew to his. She impatiently wiped away her tears. "I don't understand. You know who I am."

His hold on her loosened, and he searched her face. "No, I don't."

She sniffed. *Why would he lie?* "Asher didn't send you? Or Ian?" He shook his head once, abruptly. She looked at him and a horrifying thought came to her. For security, he was wearing a very expensive suit. "You're not a bodyguard, are you?"

His silence was answer enough.

She covered her face with one hand, even though it made her head spin. "I'm sorry. I thought my brothers had hired you." She opened her eyes and stepped back from him. This time he let her go. She stumbled then righted herself, avoiding the hand he held out to steady her. "I should have stuck with the fruity drinks."

Somehow he had her dress over her head and on her before she could protest. He picked up her shoes and took her elbow in one hand. "I'll walk you back."

She almost said she was fine, but she had the feeling he

would do exactly as he pleased, regardless of what she said. As they walked together, she said, "I don't drink anymore." Her voice caught in her throat as the emotion from earlier threatened to resurface. She didn't lose control, didn't put herself in dangerous situations—not anymore.

In the harsh tone he'd used earlier, he said, "I don't care, so you don't have to lie to me."

"I'm not lying." She stumbled again as she walked. A glance at him revealed he clearly didn't believe her. She wanted to tell him his opinion of her didn't matter, but her mouth suddenly went dry and her stomach churned in warning. She paused and wrapped an arm around a palm tree.

His hand tightened on her elbow. "No stopping now. We're almost there."

"I feel a little—"

"You'll be fine tomorrow. I'll have someone make sure you get a glass of water and some aspirin. Which part of the hotel are you staying in? Do you have your key with you?"

Kenzi felt at her side. "Shit, I left my purse at the bar." She sank to her knees on one side of the path. The man beside her and the fate of her purse were of little consequence as she fought back the urge to retch. She heard him greet someone; they sounded so far away, even though they were beside her.

A man said, "Is everything all right?"

"Does it look all right?"

"How can I help?"

"Call a doctor and help me get her to her room."

"She's probably staying in the Presidential Suite. We can go through the side entrance."

"You know her?"

"Not personally, but I recognize her from photos. Kenzi Barrington. Her brother is Asher Barrington, from Boston. I met them through the Hendersons once."

"What the hell is she doing here?"

"Right now? Throwing up on your shoe."

"Fuck."

A moment later, Kenzi felt a cold, wet towel pressed into her hands. She stood shakily and gave herself over to the strong arms that supported her as she walked into the hotel. Once inside, she felt like she was floating when he picked her up and carried her into the elevator. She laid her head on the strong shoulder beneath the expensive suit. The storm had passed, and she was coasting on the lovely numbness she'd sought.

This. This is good enough to make me forget.

After a moment (or was it several?), she heard a woman instruct her to lift her arms, and she did so obediently. She slid into the most heavenly bed and closed her eyes. A quick annoyance of a pill and a glass of water followed, then she fell back against the pillows again.

"Does she need a hospital?"

The woman answered, "In my opinion, no. She'll have quite a hangover, though."

"Call me when she wakes up."

"Absolutely, Mr. Marshall."

"And your discretion with this matter will be rewarded."

"I understand, Mr. Marshall."

Kenzi's eyes fluttered open. She sought the eyes of the man she'd briefly fancied earlier. If there had ever been a spark between them, she'd certainly extinguished it. The thought made her sad, even though she had no idea who he was. One more opportunity gone before being explored. She croaked, "I'm sorry about your shoes."

He stood next to the bed, his expression unreadable. "Why are you here?"

She answered honestly. "Islands make me happy. The waves wash everything away."

He frowned but didn't say anything.

Kenzi shrugged beneath the blankets. "Usually. But not this time. That's why I tried the rum."

An angry expression twisted his features. "What do you need to forget?"

"Everything," Kenzi said and closed her eyes, letting herself slip into the deep sleep the alcohol had been pulling her toward.

MORNING COFFEE DIDN'T help Dax's sour mood. The long, early-morning run he'd taken on the beach hadn't either. After his shower, he checked his phone to see if he'd missed a message, but he hadn't. He made several business calls then checked his messages again.

Kenzi Barrington.

If she were dead, someone would have called.

He picked up his cell phone to call Clay Landon, who had helped him get Kenzi back to her room. Clay was one of the few people he trusted. They had been friends for a long time, and he'd brought him along to the Bahamas because resorts were not Dax's usual acquisition. He'd offered Clay a slice of the profit, but, as usual, Clay had refused to accept it. Dax had a hard time understanding what motivated Clay at times. He was insanely rich but lived a relatively modest lifestyle. He was brilliant but hadn't applied that intelligence to any substantial project. He dabbled in real estate and the stock market, pretty much anything that promised to hold his attention for more than five minutes. There were times Dax had wondered if Clay considered him a good friend merely because he found Dax interesting.

The bane of a poor man is starvation.

The bane of a rich man—boredom.

Clay could probably afford to feed a nation and would if someone convinced him it wouldn't be a tediously boring prospect.

So when a rumor had surfaced that one of the largest family-owned resorts in the Caribbean was teetering financially, it had been irresistible blood in the water to a shark like Dax and a tempting distraction for Clay. Dax had closed the deal the night before, but optimizing the profit by reselling to developers was Clay's area of expertise. He looked at this acquisition as he did all of his others: a means to an end. Unlike Clay, Dax stayed to one course. Life was about knowing what one wanted, taking pleasure or profit where it presented itself, then moving on.

He didn't get bored nor did he get excited about much. Wealth was the only sustainable constant he believed in.

People were fickle. Companies rose and fell. Trends changed. Wealth was power, and power was all that mattered. He surrounded himself with people who understood how little tolerance he had for sentimentality. More than once, his friends had told him he was too honest, brutally honest was what they called him, but lies required a person to care about what others thought, and Dax didn't care.

He lived life on his terms—no excuses, no regrets.

And when it came to business takeovers—no mercy.

Although he was bold, he wasn't reckless. He had enemies, but was smart when dealing with them. Liking or hating competition was a waste of time. Neither emotion moved a buyout forward. Business was business. Nothing personal. The less drama, the better.

The media didn't follow him, because he kept his private life extremely private. The deadliest animals in the wild disguised themselves to match their surroundings. Maintaining a low profile meant he didn't get involved in anything that didn't directly affect his business. Last night, Kenzi Barrington had looked as if she might. She'd walked past him, and something about her expression had caught his attention.

He told himself he'd followed her only because a beach drowning had never increased the value of any property. Nor would it be good for business to have to explain to a family like the Barringtons that their youngest had met her end while staying at a resort he now owned.

It had been more than that, though, and he was at a loss to explain it. She'd drawn him to the beach and held him entranced. His fascination with her was impossible to justify to himself the next day. She was beautiful, but lust hadn't been what he'd felt when he'd followed her. As he'd stood watching her walk, he'd experienced the strangest sensation that he was supposed to be there with her.

There was a chance her presence at the resort was linked to the next project on his calendar. When Trent Davis had approached him as a possible buyer for the Henderson's company, he had put Poly-Shyn on Dax's radar. Dax had looked into it, but at the time, the company had been stable. No fast money could be made there. However, fighting within the Henderson family over the future of the company had caused its stock to plummet, and it was now ripe for forced takeover. So far, Dax hadn't done more than explore his options. Had the Hendersons sent a family friend to covertly uncover his level of interest in the project?

Clay picked up after a few rings. "Dax, you'll be happy to know I smoothed things over with the Barrington woman. I went over early with a Bloody Mary and breakfast, laid on the Landon charm, and then sent her home in my private jet. She was embarrassed but not upset when she left. She probably doesn't even remember getting sick. You can thank me with a fabulous lunch after we videoconference with a buyer today at noon. Max Andrade called me."

Leave it to Clay to get involved out of what had likely been nothing more than curiosity. "You sent her home?" His question surprised even him.

"Did you hear me? Max Andrade. That's a solid buyer, if we can sell him on the property. He'll want to keep it as a resort, and that would mean less time invested in dealing with permits and demolition. You could get in and out, and make a killing if you do this right."

Dax rubbed one of his pounding temples. *Focus.* "You've dealt with Max in the past. How do we play this?"

"He'll come in with a low offer. He always does, but if he sees potential in the area, he has the funds to meet your profit goal. With him, the price doesn't matter as much as getting what he wants. I'll pressure Hurd to put in an offer quickly, and we'll apply some pressure. Tourist trap or Silicon Valley tax shelter: You don't have a preference, do you?"

"None," Dax answered automatically. He told himself he was relieved Clay had dealt with the Barrington woman. There was no need for him to see her again.

Still, he couldn't shake the image of how desperate she'd looked just before she'd fallen asleep.

"Don't touch me."

He'd been trying to help her for God's sake.

She'd looked terrified . . .

"Don't touch me."

Had someone hurt her?

The idea of it filled him with rage. He'd love to have five minutes alone with whoever had put that fear in her.

Hell, killing didn't require that much time.

Dax shook his head. *What the hell am I thinking? I don't know her, and her issues are none of my concern.*

"You don't sound excited. What's wrong with you this morning?"

Dax rubbed his temple again. "I'm fighting something."

"Good. I don't mean good that you might be sick, but good that it's not what I thought. For a minute there, I thought you might be mooning over the Barrington woman. She is one hot mess, even sober. Sweet, but I can see why she's not married."

"Shut the fuck up about her. Understand?"

"Uh-oh. You liked her, didn't you? I saw it in your face last night. Do yourself a favor, Dax, and stay the hell away from that one."

"Be here at noon, and we'll use my laptop to conference with Max." He took a deep, calming breath. "And thanks for handling everything this morning."

Clay cleared his throat. "You're welcome, but proceed with caution, my friend. And I'm not talking about Max."

Dax rolled his eyes in frustration. "I have no intention of seeing her again."

"I know," Clay said in a voice laden with irony, "but don't say I didn't warn you."

Chapter Two

P LANES AND HANGOVERS don't mix. Not even private jets. Kenzi had done her best to sleep on the flight, but she collapsed into the back of the town car that met her at the airport and didn't dare check a mirror. She knew she looked how she felt, like shit.

Her phone beeped as messages piled up on her cell phone. She didn't have to check them to know who they'd be from. Her mother and father would be first, followed by her brother Ian, who would deliver a request for her to call home because her absence, even when announced, worried her parents. One by one, her other brothers would follow suit and deliver the same message with their own personal flair. Grant would be worried about her but even more about how she was upsetting their mother. Asher would order her as if she worked for him. Lance would lay out all the reasons why calling was the best for all involved. She wouldn't hear from Andrew if he was deployed, and he was, but when he was home, he joined the phone chain along with the rest of them. He threw in his tediously long lecture about duty and loyalty.

I'm twenty-eight years old. I should be able to go more than two days without talking to my parents before my family dives into crisis mode.

Even when her parents had sent her away to an all girls' private high school in Nova Scotia she'd had to check in with them twice a day or they lost their minds. There was a sad irony in that for her. *Why send me to study in another country but expect me to check in like I'm living under your roof?*

Because you don't trust me to make decisions for myself.

That's nothing new.

Kenzi opened her eyes and looked at the driver. The wire coming from his ear fit with the military cut of his hair. "Are you from Platinum Transportation?"

"No, ma'am. My name is Parker Draun. Your family hired me before you left the country, but unfortunately I was unable to locate you prior to your departure."

Kenzi closed her eyes again and laid her head back on the seat. Was the man who he said he was? What proof did she have that he wasn't a kidnapper? A crazy murderer? Was this how she'd meet her end?

I should be so lucky.

No, she corrected herself, *I don't want to die. I just don't know if I can live the lie anymore.*

She knew there were people who had endured worse than she had, but that saddened her instead of making her feel better. *Think about something else. Anything else. Something good.*

She thought about the man she'd met the night before

and the assumptions she'd made about him. Her memories of the night were sketchy, but she remembered how he'd made her feel.

People joked that beer goggles made everyone attractive.

Rum goggles were apparently even more potent.

Not that the feeling had been mutual. *Nothing says, "I'm not interested" like sending someone else the next morning to handle my departure.*

What did I expect? A call to see how I was doing? He didn't even tell me his name. His friend had to do that.

Dax Marshall.

Even his name is sexy.

Take me, Dax.

Do me, Dax.

I wonder if that's his real name or if his parents had saddled him with something like Erwin, but he wasn't getting laid because no one wanted to scream that name out?

Who am I kidding? He could be named Watch-Out-I-Have-a-Rash and women would sleep with him. He was hot.

And I'd been drunk. Oh, so drunk.

Thank God nothing happened.

At least, I'm ninety-nine percent certain nothing did.

Although, I do remember taking my dress off.

Kenzi cringed. *Then he put it back on. Yeah, that's a sign if ever there was one.*

So much for using that memory to make me feel better.

Without opening her eyes Kenzi took out her phone and said, "Willa." The best cure for her mood was to talk with a good friend. Willa Chambers and her twin sister, Lexi, had been Kenzi's best friends since they'd met in boarding school. They'd seen her through some rough years and never pushed her to explain what had fueled her bad choices. Even though they were her age, she often turned to them as someone would to older sisters. Although they'd claimed their decision to move to Boston had been job related, she knew the truth. They loved her as much as she loved them. She couldn't imagine her life without them.

"Kenzi, how was your trip? Do you feel better?"

"Much," Kenzi lied.

"I know how important that reality show was to you. Have you talked to your family about it yet? Maybe you can convince them to reconsider."

"Not worth it. I'm over it."

"I don't believe that for a second."

Kenzi sighed. "It was a silly idea, anyway. I've never seen my mother as happy as she has been lately. She's planning Asher and Emily's wedding, helping Emily prepare for the opening of her museum, and picking out names for their children. Why would I want to do anything that could threaten that?"

"That's a lot of *Emily*."

"Having her around has been good for my mother. I'm happy Asher found her."

"Liar."

"I'm trying, Willa. Isn't that good enough?"

"You have to pretend with them, but you don't have to with me. Remember what you said to Lexi and me when we asked you how you could tell us apart when no one else could? You said it's because you see us. US. Not just our features or how we dress. Well, I see you, Kenzi. And I'm not your mother. You don't have to watch everything you say to me. So you don't love your future sister-in-law. So what? She practically moved in with your parents for a while. I don't know how I'd feel if my parents tossed me out in my teens but took in some strange woman like she was their long-lost daughter."

"Easy on the understanding, Willa; it's not making me feel better." Kenzi sat up and stretched. "I don't dislike Emily. It's not her fault my family is fucked up."

"So, what will you do now?"

"Maybe nothing. I don't have to work. My trust fund can support me."

"First, when you talk like that I want to slap you. It's really hard for me to pity you when you go all sad-rich-girl on me. Second, you're not a child anymore. You can make your own decisions now. If you want to do a reality show, take some of that trust fund and film it yourself."

"My family would never let it be seen."

"Blah. Blah. Blah. Excuses. If you want this, Kenzi, fight for it. Tell your story."

"No matter who it hurts?"

"Whatever you're holding in is tearing you apart, Kenzi."

"There are things I've never told you, Willa." Sober, Kenzi pushed back the dark memories that threatened to wash over her at the mere mention of that time. It was a battle she'd fought and won within herself countless times in the past.

"And you never have to, unless you want to. Those who love you will stand with you when you tell your story, and those who don't—you don't need them."

Kenzi brought a shaking hand to her mouth. Willa made it sound so easy. "I don't know if I can risk being the reason my mother suffers more than she already has."

"Your mother will survive."

"Ian will never forgive me if it affects his political career."

"He loves you. He'll work it out. He always does."

"How can you be so sure about what I should do when my head is pounding from nerves just at the thought of hiring my own film team?"

"Oh, that's easy, because I'm looking on instead of facing this myself. In the end, Kenzi, it doesn't matter what I think. Do what you can live with. I'll love you, regardless."

Kenzi wiped away a stray tear that ran down her cheek. How many times had she yearned to hear those words from her parents or brothers? Too many. Although Willa's speech had been inspiring, Kenzi wasn't sold on going forward with the show herself.

After so many years of keeping everything inside so she wouldn't upset anyone, could she defy her family and expose her pain to the world? Wouldn't it be better to continue to bury the memories, push past how she felt, and choose the welfare of her family over her selfish desire to be heard?

How long can I pretend I'm fine before I shatter beneath the weight of the truth?

After hanging up with Willa, Kenzi rode the rest of the way to her Boston apartment in silence. Her driver parked then escorted her to her door.

"I'll be out here if you need me," he said.

"Of course you will be," Kenzi said with a sad smile and closed the door between them. Almost instantly, she whipped the door back open and said, "I'll pay you double whatever my family offered if you don't tell them anything you see me do or say."

The man looked at her long and hard until she was sure he'd refuse. Then he said, "My normal fee is fine. I'll bill you instead and sign a non-disclosure."

Surprised at how easy that had gone, Kenzi asked, "How much would it cost for you to stop following me around?"

A faint smile curled the man's lips. "They'd only send someone else."

"What if you simply promise that I won't see you?"

He nodded in agreement.

"Do you have a family?"

"Yes, ma'am. A wife and two kids."

"Are they in Boston?"

"Bellingham."

"Do you like your job?"

"It pays the bills and allows me to save some on the side. My wife can stay home if she wants. Between my shifts my brother, Josh, will be with you."

"You're in business with your brother?"

"Since we shook kids down for their lunch money together in kindergarten."

"You're joking."

"Yes, ma'am."

"Call me Kenzi." Kenzi let out a long breath. She knew what she was doing. It was how she'd always survived. She looked for something to like when situations were otherwise intolerable and clung to it. It was how she'd kept her silence as long as she had. She knew how to bury how she felt and focus on one small good thing as if it were a treasure. "I look forward to meeting your brother."

Parker nodded and turned his back in a stance that said he'd be stationed outside her door. As if he couldn't stop himself from saying it, he added, "Your family hired me because they care about you. At the end of the day, family is all that really matters."

Kenzi nodded and closed the door. She rested against it for a moment. *That's what I keep telling myself, but it's not that simple.*

A short time later Kenzi was stretching on her yoga mat when the bellman called up, saying she'd received a delivery. She told him to send it up. She opened the door and cocked her head to the side when she received a wrapped gift box. She placed it on the coffee table in her living room and opened the card that accompanied it.

"You are stronger than whatever you are facing. Dax Marshall," she read aloud.

With shaking hands, Kenzi unwrapped the gift he had sent. It was an iPod. She turned it on and saw it came with music preloaded. She hit play and the sound of ocean waves filled her living room.

She didn't ask herself why he'd sent the gift. She didn't want to think about how a man who didn't know her at all knew her so well. She curled up on her couch, gave herself over to the tears she'd held in for so long, and let the sound of the waves wash them away as they always had.

She fell asleep, and it was the most peaceful sleep she'd had in a long time.

SEVERAL DAYS LATER, Dax was back in his London office, snapping at everyone who had the misfortune of walking through his door. Jetlag didn't normally bother him, but he hadn't slept well since he'd returned from the Bahamas. He should be in a better mood. Negotiations with Max Andrade were progressing and promising. He was readying himself to turn his attention back to the matter of Poly-Shyn.

A question was eating at him, though, and he finally gave in to it. He walked into his secretary's office and asked, "Kate, did you track the package I had you send?"

Kate was in her late twenties and single, but she didn't bring her personal life into the office, and Dax didn't normally involve her in his. She had, however, handled his detailed request for Kenzi's gift without hesitation. She looked down quickly and checked her computer. "I did. It arrived that day and was signed for."

"By Miss Barrington?"

"No, a man. She probably has someone receive packages for her."

Dax frowned as he snapped, "Then how do I know if she actually got it?"

"Would you like me to call her and confirm delivery?"

"No, I would not," Dax growled and walked back into

his office, slamming the door behind him.

Checking to see if Kenzi had received his gift would open a door that was better left closed. He'd only sent the iPod because he couldn't get the last thing she said to him out of his head. She was obviously a troubled woman. Clay saw it as clearly as he had. Whatever had happened to her, or was happening to her, was none of his business. She certainly wasn't alone in the world. Hell, she had more family than most women had shoes.

Still, he was restless in the face of her unhappiness, and it was distracting him. He wasn't a man who sent presents, not even to women he dated, but he'd wanted her to know he'd heard her.

Ridiculous.

She probably wants to forget her drunken ramblings as much as I wish I could.

Dax sat down at his desk and glared at his phone. *Is a fucking thank you so hard?*

He opened the file on his desk that contained her contact information and a brief background check on her. There was no great tragedy leaping off the pages. Nothing.

He slammed the file shut.

Forget about her. Focus on the resort and Poly-Shyn.

Nothing else matters.

Chapter Three

KENZI CAUGHT HER reflection in the glass that flanked the door of her parents' home and paused. Her makeup matched her attire, subdued elegance. Silk blouse and matching slacks both tailored to a classic rather than a trendy cut. Her hair was neatly tied back. With armor fully in place, she forced a smile she'd cultivated from early childhood. Her oldest brother's fiancée, Emily, loved game night and her father said that was part of the reason her mother was doing so well.

So suck it up, Kenzi. Look happy.

Her father, Dale, opened the door. "Kenzi, we were starting to think you'd fallen off the planet."

Kenzi greeted her father with a kiss on the cheek. How she felt wasn't his fault either. He was just as much a prisoner of circumstance as she was. He'd given up a career for her mother, Sophie, but his love for her was one thing Kenzi never doubted. "I meant to call you back. Sorry. Things came up and I . . ." Her voice trailed off when she met her father's eyes. She'd never been good at lying to him. "I needed a few days on my own."

Dale closed the door behind her and took her coat. "You know how your mother worries when she doesn't hear from you."

Kenzi forced a placating smile to her lips. "I'm here now and ready for a night of Monopoly or charades."

Dale studied his daughter's face for a moment. "Is there something upsetting you?"

Kenzi almost said yes, then she reined her honesty back. Her father didn't want to know the truth. *Wait for it. Wait for it.*

He continued, "Because your mother is so happy lately. Let's have a peaceful night."

And there it is, the reason he asked if I'm okay. Not because he wants to know how I feel, but because he doesn't want me to ruin game night with messy emotions or inconvenient anger.

One kind of lie came easily because it had been told so many times. "I'm fine, Dad. I wouldn't be here if I weren't."

Dale pressed his lips together as if he wanted to say something but changed his mind. Then he said, "Game night is fun, isn't it? It's good for you to be spending time with your brothers and laughing."

Gotcha: don't forget to laugh. She linked arms with her father and started toward the living room with him. "Is everyone here already? And what's on the calendar? Cards? Scrabble? *A piñata?*"

Her father paused and looked at her for a long moment.

Kenzi gave herself a mental shake. *Whoops. Sorry, didn't mean to let my feelings show there.*

"Kenzi—"

"I know, Dad. Sorry."

They started walking again and, as they entered the living room, Sophie rose and rushed over to hug her warmly. "Kenzi, I'm so glad you're here."

She wasn't angry, and that added to Kenzi's guilt. Kenzi might hate the circumstances that had changed Sophie; she could resent how fragile tragedy had left her mother and what that meant for their family—but Sophie herself? She was the single kindest, most loving person Kenzi had ever met. Hating her would be like hating a puppy for wanting to cuddle on your lap. "How could I miss game night?"

Emily waved from the couch. Kenzi waved back. Asher nodded from where he was standing, talking to Ian.

Lance, the brother closest to her age, came over and put an arm around her shoulder. "You're on my team tonight. Have you ever played Scattergories? Looks like that's the poison of the evening." Kenzi's eyes flew to his. He quickly said, "I'm kidding; it sounds fun."

Whether he meant it or had said it to appease those who were listening, Kenzi didn't know. It didn't matter either way. The line between truth and forced reality had blurred a long time ago. "Does it matter which game we play as long as we kick a little ass?"

"Kenzi—" her father said in soft reprimand at her curse.

Asher laughed and said, "That's the spirit, Kenzi. I knew there was a scrapper in you. Tell us how you really feel."

Kenzi looked around the room at the happy expressions on everyone's faces and imagined how quickly the evening would change if she actually said what was bubbling within her.

You want to know the truth?

I hate that you do whatever you want no matter what I say.

I hate that you canceled my show.

I hate that I can't tell you how angry I am.

Why can't we ever talk about how we feel?

I want to say his name.

I want to tell you I'm not the perfect daughter or the perfect sister you think I am. I want to lay all my ugly secrets at your feet and see if you still love me.

Kenzi took a deep breath and pushed those thoughts away. *Stop being selfish.* No, they didn't love her the unconditional way she yearned for, but they weren't bad people. Maybe they, like her, were surviving the only way they knew how.

Was game night good for them?

If we suffer through enough of these, like bad-tasting medicine, will we come out on the other side healthier?

After years of gathering for holidays and during their annual April week of denial, they were now gathering at least twice a month with the goal of simply enjoying each other's company. Kenzi looked at Emily who was smiling warmly at her. Instead of feeling threatened by her, Kenzi told herself she should be grateful to her.

Find the good. Focus on that. Emily makes Asher happy. She makes my parents happy. She'll probably be a wonderful mother for my nephews and nieces when they come.

I can do this. I can leave well enough alone.

Kenzi squared her shoulders and shook a fist playfully in

the air. "I feel victory coming, that's all I feel. Let's get this game started."

A laugh spread through the room, and they all sat down to play. As Emily explained the rules of the game, Kenzi pushed herself to enjoy the evening until she had almost convinced even herself she had.

She claimed she had an early morning the next day and left her parents' home after the second round of Scattergories. It had been a successful evening measured by the level of happiness it had brought Sophie. They would get together again in a couple weeks and by then Kenzi was determined to be in a better state of mind.

She said good night to Josh at the door of her apartment, walked inside, and kicked off her shoes. She plopped onto the couch, leaned forward to pick up the iPod, and hit play. She sat back against the cushions and let the soothing sound of waves wash over her.

A small part of her felt guilty for not calling Dax Marshall to thank him for the gift. She could hear her father's voice telling her he'd raised her with better manners than that. Calling Dax, though, would have forced her to face why he'd sent her the gift in the first place.

I can only imagine what I must have said to him for him to send this.

She'd considered throwing away the gift to help wipe that night completely away, but she couldn't. There was something about the message he'd sent along with the gift that made her feel less alone. It wasn't only the sound of the ocean that soothed her; it was the fantasy that the man who'd sent it to her cared about her and how she felt.

He'd heard her.

She wasn't ready to replace that fantasy with whatever truth she would discover during an actual conversation with Dax. He could have sent it out of guilt over something he'd said to her. Guilt was a powerful motivator. It always made her otherwise independent and powerful brothers drop everything when their father called. It was why Kenzi had moved back to Boston.

Not guilt. I like my version better. She held the iPod to her chest and closed her eyes, savoring the memory of Dax. Memories of the night were sketchy, but she would never forget how strong his arms had felt when he'd held her against him. The light scent of his cologne. It was one she recognized, and normally mildly liked, but on Dax it was heavenly. Her body hummed with excitement from the memory of being near him. It wasn't like that most of the time. Usually she couldn't put the past behind her long enough to think of a man that way.

I should thank him.

For the gift, not for my wayward thoughts.

She picked up her phone and did a quick Internet search. He had offices in several cities. She randomly chose one of them and decided to send him something small along with an acknowledgment that she'd received his gift.

No need to talk to him. No need to face the truth. *Just a quick thank you, and it's done.*

ANOTHER WEEK PASSED and Dax had mostly pushed Kenzi

out of his head. He'd stopped waiting for a response from her, stopped wondering why she hadn't contacted him, and had taken two different women out on dates to prove to himself that he didn't care if she ever did.

Oddly, the evenings had consisted only of dinner.

No sex, even though both had shown interest.

Kate buzzed in on his desk intercom. "Mr. Maxwell Andrade is on line one. Should I put him through?"

"I'll do it."

Work, the perfect cure to all ailments. Dax hit a button on his telephone and said, "Max, I was just looking over your offer."

"Good," Max said in the crisp tone that was his norm. "But that's not why I called."

"Really?" Dax leaned back in his chair. Their conversations to that point had revolved solely around the island property. "How can I help you?"

"I met with Trent Davis, and he mentioned speaking to you regarding Poly-Shyn."

"He did."

"Circumstances have changed since he spoke with you."

"They certainly have. The company isn't worth nearly what they were asking."

"Poly-Shyn is no longer going to be sold. The youngest son wants it."

"Dean Henderson? He'll lose it in a card game if he gets it. The family should consider anything I give them a gift if that's their plan for it. What's your interest in this?"

"My family protects its own. The Hendersons are friends

of the family."

Dax drummed his fingers on the table.

Max continued, "It would mean a lot to my family if you turn your attention elsewhere."

Dax could have told him that his interest in the company was at the preliminary stage, but he didn't like Max's tone. "I'm afraid that's not how I do business."

"Let me make this clearer. If you do anything that adversely affects the Hendersons, you'll quickly regret it."

"Is that a threat?"

"It's a promise, and consider my bid for your resort retracted."

"Do what you need to do. Shame about the Bahamas. It had Andrade written all over it."

"I don't think you understand how ugly this could get."

Dax dismissed the final threat. "Ring me if you change your mind." With that, he hung up.

The loss of a buyer for the property hadn't fazed him. What Max Andrade had not yet learned was that no matter how good a person or an opportunity appeared, they were always replaceable. Always.

The conversation, however, had sealed the fate for Poly-Shyn.

He could profit from taking over countless other teetering companies—each with less chance of being a professional landmine—but Dax's course was set. If Max hadn't laced his request with a threat, who knows, maybe Dax could have been swayed. Instead, Max had hit him on his Achilles heel.

No one told him what to do.

He had worked too hard to put himself in a position where no one could.

A shadow of a memory from his childhood surged within him, and he slammed a fist on his desk. His father had lived large, partied hard, and died before his time while flying his fourth wife to Europe for cosmetic surgery, leaving a young and angry Dax in the custody of an uncle who thought discipline was best delivered with a fist. He'd had no respect for how Dax's father had lived and had said it was his duty to make a man out of Dax.

Dax had never known his mother, and his uncle said she didn't matter. People who left didn't matter. Having been part of stepfamilies that had come together during his father's brief marriages only to dissolve after divorces, Dax didn't need much convincing that his uncle was right. Even though his uncle's love had been brutal, Dax told himself it had been necessary. If Dax had never felt powerless, he would have remained as weak as his father. Instead, he'd learned to channel his anger and protect himself.

When his uncle had died suddenly from a heart attack while Dax was away in college, that event, too, had shaped the man Dax had become. The inheritance he'd received from both his uncle and his father had bankrolled his first company takeover and set him free.

No one controlled Dax now.

No one ever would again.

Dax turned in his chair and stood. He'd anticipated the Barringtons coming to the defense of the Hendersons, but the Andrades were a surprise. He hadn't realized the families were that close.

Normally, he knew better than to let business become personal, but that's what this deal had become. Dax ran a hand through his hair before returning to his desk. He was frustrated. Angry. *Is this about what Max said or the fact that I haven't heard from a woman I'd be better off forgetting? I need to get her out of my head.* He stretched and turned his attention to his email.

The next day was more of the same until Kate walked into his office and announced, "Mr. Marshall, there is a package here for you."

"Put it aside; I'll look at it before I leave."

"You may want to see it now. It was sent over from the Boston office. It says it's from Miss Barrington."

Dax surged to his feet. "Bring it in."

Kate placed it on his desk with a smile. She looked as if she expected him to open it in front of her. Dax cleared his throat, and she said, "Oh, I'm sorry. I'll be at my desk if you need me."

He raised an eyebrow in question.

She smiled wider. "In case you need her phone number or to send her something else." Looking far too pleased with herself, she closed the door behind her.

Once alone, Dax picked up the small box and bounced it in his hand. It had been nearly two weeks since he'd sent Kenzi the iPod. What would she have sent him?

He read the note attached to it: *Thank you for your kind gift. Kenzi Barrington.*

Polite. Impersonal. Disappointing.

Impatient, he tore the wrapping off the gift and frowned at the contents. She'd sent him a bottle of his favorite cologne.

It was an oddly intimate and exciting gift. It instantly brought back a memory of how delectable she'd smelled and how he'd tried to deny his attraction to her when he'd carried her in the elevator. She'd buried her face in his collar, and he'd chastised his cock for confusing her nuzzling with foreplay. Apparently not even a little vomit and a few crazy outbursts could kill the boner he'd gotten from being near her. It wasn't something he was particularly proud of.

Nor was he happy with the fact that his cock was twitching with excitement at the idea that she might be remembering how it felt to be in his arms. Remembering his touch, his scent. Wishing, as he did, that the evening had ended differently.

He kept the bottle of cologne in his hand and paced his office. He could call her, but a check of his watch confirmed it was still early enough in London that Kenzi would probably still be sleeping.

In bed. He remembered how beautiful she'd looked in her panties and bra when she'd stood and stripped her dress off on the beach. He imagined how those perfect breasts of hers would look loose beneath a silk nightgown or bared to him as she arched them toward his mouth.

The front of his pants tightened again. He returned to desk, put the bottle in one of his drawers, and tried to return his focus to his email. He somewhat succeeded, and the next few hours quickly passed.

The door of his office flew open and Clay barged in with a flustered, apologetic Kate at his heels. "I tried to get him to wait."

Dax stood and waved her away. "I know. Close the door behind you." He motioned for Clay to take a seat and sat across from him. It was easy enough to see that his friend wasn't happy. "What are you doing on this side of the pond?"

"I had business in New York. Lucky for you I did. I met with Max Andrade. What the hell, Dax? He was just about to sign. Now Hurd pulled back his offer. Didn't even lower it. Just pulled out. What happened?"

Dax folded his arms across his chest. "Max wanted me to back off of the Poly-Shyn deal."

"I didn't realize the Andrades even knew the Hendersons."

"I didn't either."

"So, he called in a personal favor. For the kind of money you were about to score on the island it might have been worth it."

"He warned me off it."

"Oh, boy. I know that tone." Clay stood, walked over to the bar in the corner of the office, and poured himself a shot of whiskey along with one for Dax. After downing his and returning to his seat, he said, "So, let me get this straight: you're going to take on three of the most powerful families on the East Coast—why? May I remind you now about your philosophy of always following the profit and not getting emotionally involved?"

"You should have heard him. He thought he could scare me."

"The Andrades are very close with Dominic Corisi."

"Dominic is barely in the game anymore. He went the way of Buffet and retired. Plus, this isn't personal. It's business."

"It sounds personal, otherwise you'd walk away."

Shit, Clay knew him too well. "No one threatens me and wins."

"There has to be more to this. Who cares what he said?"

Dax downed his own shot. He didn't care about what Max thought. This was about how the threat made Dax feel. He'd vowed that no one would ever push him down or threaten him again. He couldn't explain it to Clay without sharing things he'd spent a lifetime keeping to himself.

Clay continued to dole out advice. "Move on. There's no profit in this, but there could be a whole lot of professional suicide involved."

"You sound like you're genuinely worried for me. Since when are you scared of a little confrontation?"

"I'm not afraid of snakes, but I'd have a healthy respect for one I see coiling back to bite my ankle."

"They won't be coming for you, so don't worry. I appreciate your help with the resort, but this is my area of expertise. Takeovers are never pretty."

Clay shook his head slowly. "I want to believe you, but I've seen you head down this road before, and it doesn't end well."

Dax flexed his shoulders in memory of the fight Clay was

referring to. A decade had passed since then, but Clay brought it up from time to time as if it were a cautionary tale Dax could learn from. He didn't understand that some urges couldn't be reasoned away; they could only be contained. "That was my fight, too. Your mistake was staying."

"My mistake was thinking it was only three guys. No, you pissed off half the bar."

"I didn't like the way they were talking to the waitress."

"I didn't say you were wrong to stand up for her, you just don't know when to cut and run."

"We gave as good as we got that night."

"But at what cost? Your face took a pounding, and I still have scars from that bottle-wielding biker."

Dax smiled without humor. "But we won."

Clay sighed. "Barely. Is that really the kind of fight you're looking for again, but with your career? I've got your back, but you know you could end this now."

Dax rubbed his hands over his face. Clay was a good friend, and he was making sense. Dax wanted to say he'd walk away from Poly-Shyn. He didn't, though. He was wrestling with an old demon, one he normally kept in check, and this time it was winning. "I'll think about it."

Clay clasped his fingers on the arms of his chair. "So, have you been up to anything else I should know about?"

Dax looked back at his desk then at Clay. He strode over, opened a drawer, pulled out the cologne, then placed it on the table beside Clay. "Kenzi Barrington sent me this. You have sisters. What does it mean?"

Clay waved a hand in the air. "No. No. No. You are not

going to battle with the Barringtons and date their little sister at the same time. If you're looking to end up on the bottom of the Charles River, you are choosing the fastest way to get yourself there."

"I'm not dating her. I sent her some music to make her feel better, and this is what she sent back. What does it mean?"

Clay stood and poured himself a second shot. "It means you've fucking lost your mind. You need to stay away from her."

"I have."

Clay downed the shot. "No, this is not staying away. This is the opposite of staying away. This is the romantic shit that is going to bring you real trouble. You want my advice?"

Dax picked up the cologne bottle and tossed it back into a drawer of his desk. Normally Dax did. Clay was the one person who had consistently looked out for Dax's best interests. That carried weight in most situations, but not in this one. When Dax asked himself why, he realized it was for no other reason than he didn't want Clay to be right. Not this time. "No."

"Walk away from all of it. Her. The takeover. Everything."

"Or?"

"Take up a religion. Any fucking religion, because you're going to need more help than I can bring."

"Isn't your motto 'It doesn't matter as long as it doesn't bore me'?"

"Ten years ago it was. I'd like to think I've evolved beyond that."

"And done what?"

"Shut the fuck up."

"Exactly."

Chapter Four

KENZI WAS WRAPPING a towel around her hair when her cell phone rang. Still damp from the shower, she walked into her bedroom to get it. She was taking calls from her family again so she no longer had to avoid her phone.

It wasn't a number she recognized, but she answered anyway. "Hello?"

"Kenzi, it's Dax Marshall."

Kenzi sank onto the edge of her bed and let out a shaky breath. "Hi." *That's me, a brilliant conversationalist.* "Did you get my gift?"

"I did."

Kenzi cleared her throat. "Was it the right brand?"

"It was."

He didn't say anything else, and Kenzi's hands went cold with nerves. What if he thought it wasn't an appropriate gift? Had his gift been one sent out of pity and her response too personal? Kenzi's stomach twisted and her mouth went dry.

She wanted to extricate herself from the conversation but they weren't actually talking, which made it that much more awkward. The longer the silence continued the less Kenzi knew what to say. She held her breath and waited.

"I'll be in Boston tomorrow," he said gruffly.

"That's great. The weather is really warming up here." *Shut up, Kenzi. He didn't call you for a weather forecast. God, it's a good thing I didn't get the reality show if this is the best I can do.*

"Come to dinner with me."

"Dinner?" Kenzi repeated. She didn't want to believe it. Didn't want to start to hope if this wasn't what she thought it was. "Like a date?"

When he didn't answer, Kenzi groaned and flopped back on the bed, covering her face with one arm. He probably wanted to see her in person to let her down gently. Kenzi spent the next unbearably long moment wondering how to turn back the clock and unask her question.

"Yes. I want to see you again." The admission sounded like it was wrung out of him.

If Kenzi hadn't already been lying down, she would have fallen to the floor. She gasped at the pleasure his words sent rushing through her. "I didn't think our first meeting had left you with a very good impression of me."

"I'll pick you up at six. Wear something I'll spend all night thinking about tearing off you." He hung up without waiting for her response.

Holy shit.

Kenzi sat straight up and called Lexi. When she needed cheering up, Willa always knew what to say. This time, however, she needed someone who knew how to handle a man like Dax.

Lexi crowed with delight when Kenzi told her why she'd called. "It's Kenzi," she exclaimed, "and she wants advice about a man."

"Put her on speakerphone," Willa demanded in the background.

"She called me, so obviously she's found herself a real man and not one of those pretty boys the two of you normally discuss."

Kenzi laughed and decided two opinions might be better than one. "You can both hear this." She started from the beginning, well as much of the beginning as she could remember, and both women listened quietly until she mentioned the gift Dax had sent her.

"That's so sweet," they said in unison.

She plowed on and said how she'd thanked him by sending a bottle of the cologne she'd smelled on him the night she'd met him.

"Genius," Willa said.

"So hot," Lexi said at the same time.

"So, when he called today, I thought he might just have been thanking me for thanking him, but he asked me out to dinner tomorrow night." *He didn't really ask me out. He more or less ordered me to be ready and dressed especially for him.*

Kenzi fanned herself with her free hand.

"That's awesome," Willa said.

"He's gorgeous," Lexi added.

Kenzi lowered her voice and couldn't stop smiling as she said, "He told me to wear something he'd spend the night thinking about tearing off me." *And the way he said it made me want him to—more than I want to admit to even myself.*

"Oh. My. God," Willa said.

"I just wet my panties," Lexi joked.

"That's disgusting," Willa reprimanded.

"Prude," Lexi countered.

"Porn-star mouth."

"Really? That's the best you could do?"

Years of friendship with them had taught Kenzi to never take how they spoke to each other seriously. They rarely actually argued, but they did love to verbally spar over almost everything. Normally their banter would have her laughing, but she had a purpose for the call. "Could we focus here? I think he likes me."

"Um, yeah," Lexi said with heavy sarcasm.

"But you shouldn't let him talk to you like that. Wear a turtleneck and nun shoes. Make a statement that he has to respect you. That's what I'd do."

"And that's why you never get laid, Willa," Lexi countered. "I have the perfect dress that will guarantee he'll walk funny all night. Our photo shoot tomorrow was canceled. Willa, let's give Kenzi a makeover. Come on. It'll be fun."

Hearing Lexi's excitement made her date with Dax that much more real. There were things about herself that she'd never felt comfortable talking about, not even with them. When they'd first met she'd still been in a self-destructive place. They'd glimpsed some of it, but she'd kept the worst of it hidden. She didn't want to talk about the past. She didn't want to be the product of her past. She wanted to enjoy this the same way any woman would, so she blocked off a part of herself and kept her voice cheerful. "I like this guy. I mean, I don't know him. I only met him when I was drunk, but what I remember was amazing."

"That sounds like every relationship Lexi has had," Willa joked. "Ouch."

Lexi added, "Don't listen to her. You called the right one of us for advice. At least I date. Ouch. Don't pinch me."

"Then don't pinch *me*."

Kenzi burst out laughing. Even something as wildly confusing as a date with a man like Dax was less scary when plotted with her best friends. "Can we compromise and come up with an outfit that is tastefully sexy?"

"I'll do your makeup," Willa promised.

"I'll bring some outfits over," Lexi said.

She felt young, sexy, and excited about seeing a man she'd been thinking about for weeks. She pushed back the memories of him throwing her dress back at her on the beach and saying he didn't care if she drank or not, implying he didn't care enough about her for it to matter. She didn't want to think about how he'd sent someone else to check in on her the morning after they'd met. No, that wasn't who she was going on a date with. The Dax Marshall she was imagining was the one who had sent her the sound of waves because he knew they calmed her. A man who had seen her at her worst, heard her, and wanted to get to know her better.

Which Dax would show up on the date?

There was only one way to know.

HIS FLIGHT TO Boston was long and exhausting. Dax usually slept, but he was too restless. His mood wasn't the best for sitting through meeting after meeting on next to no sleep. He met with several US department heads, checked in globally on a variety of projects and, in general, tried not to watch the clock. He told himself business was the main reason for his trip, and dinner with Kenzi was merely a bonus. He attributed his inattention to fatigue.

He read a brief on the latest state of Poly-Shyn but tabled taking action on it. If he did move forward, he wanted the decision to be based on the numbers and not whatever was twisting his insides up. He forced himself to plow through back-to-back phone calls before conceding to himself that his office was the last place he wanted to be.

Late afternoon, he informed his office staff he was leaving early. He didn't explain and they didn't ask. They were likely relieved that, unlike his last visit to the Boston office, their own workday wouldn't be extended along with his past midnight. They probably thought he was off to a business dinner given how his state-side personal life was nonexistent. Whenever he came to Boston, he was all business.

Until Kenzi.

He showered and changed into a new suit with a speed he attributed to efficiency rather than admitting he was impatient to see Kenzi again. He stood in front of a full-length mirror and for once didn't like what he saw. His suit had been tailored to fit him by arguably the best men's clothing designer in London, but it didn't look right. He remembered how Kenzi had confused him with a hired bodyguard, and he could see why. He never dressed down, not even for a celebratory walk of the grounds of an island resort. He looked stiff.

He removed his tie and unbuttoned the top button on his shirt. Kenzi was close to his age, but she had a younger air about her.

Dax met his eyes in the mirror and shook his head in amused disgust. *Look at me, worried if some woman will find me attractive. What, am I back in high school? She's probably nothing like I remember her.* Weeks of thinking about her had given his imagination free rein to enhance her beauty. There was no way he would find her figure as perfect as he remembered. Her eyes would never be as easy to lose himself in. The pull she had over him would soon be shown to have been exaggerated.

For all I know, she'll be drunk again tonight, and how I look will be irrelevant.

Unless she'd been honest that night and it really was a one-time aberration because she needed to forget something.

Which would also make how I look unimportant. If she's scared or running from something, I won't take advantage of that.

In summation, there is very little chance sex is on the menu.

Then what the hell am I doing here?

He couldn't answer that question, so he didn't try. He turned away from the mirror and gathered up his wallet and phone. Seeing her again would prove once and for all that she was no different from every other woman he'd known.

Only then would things go back to normal.

He impulsively ordered his driver to stop a few blocks from her apartment when he saw a street vendor selling roses, but when the driver waited for instructions, he gave none. Dax wasn't the type who brought flowers. He took women to dinner or to a social event. Sometimes the evening ended with a romp in her bed, but it wasn't something he put much thought into. Sex was as natural as breathing, and he'd always felt sorry for those who had to dress it up as more to engage in it.

Like his father who had married practically every woman he'd fucked. Vows meant nothing. Flowers meant even less. He knew many men who sent dozens of roses when they felt bad about screwing someone besides their wife. *Skip the foliage and keep your dick in your pants.*

The idea of entering into anything that would lead to sending a forgive-me-for-not-wanting-to-fuck-only-you bouquet was enough to have Dax waving the driver to keep going.

"Are you sure, sir?" the driver asked.

"Yes," Dax said firmly.

The driver pulled back into traffic, and they rode in silence until he parked in front of Kenzi's apartment building. He walked around to open Dax's door and Dax got out but stood for a long moment simply staring at the building.

Kenzi was a complicated woman, and he didn't like complicated. She was troubled, and he avoided emotional situations. If she needed a soft shoulder to cry on, she wouldn't find one with him. Life had hardened him. He had little patience for his own emotions, never mind anyone else's. He studied the windows above and wondered which was hers.

I need to know she's okay.

He walked up the stone steps, into the foyer, and pressed the button beneath her name. When she answered her voice was breathless and excited.

"Hello?"

"I'm downstairs."

"Okay, come on up. Unless you want me to come down. Of course you do. Why would you want to come up when we're leaving right away? I'll come down." She sounded adorably flustered.

Sexy and feminine.

Fuck.

Dax tensed. He stood there impatiently waiting for her like some schoolboy on his first date. When the elevator doors opened and he saw the little black dress and those beautifully bare legs that went on for miles, he swallowed hard. The higher his eyes traveled, the tighter the crotch of his pants became on his swelling cock. The neckline of the dress dipped low enough to reveal a swell of breasts, deep enough for him to wonder if she'd worn a bra.

He groaned.

I told her to wear something I'd spend all night wanting to tear off her.

I'm a fucking masochist.

Chapter Five

DAX WATCHED KENZI so intensely she hoped she didn't trip as she walked toward him. He didn't rush forward to greet her when she walked out of the elevator, but there was a fire in his eyes and a hint of a smile on his lips. Kenzi came to a stop about a foot in front of him. She'd meant to stop sooner, but as she tilted her head back to look up at him, she admitted to herself he was a temptation she wanted to give in to.

She bit her bottom lip and waited for him to say something. When he didn't, she enjoyed the way her body hummed simply by being close to him. Exactly as she remembered, but better. There was no confusion this time. No wondering if how she felt was being enhanced by inebriation. No, regardless of how little sense it made, her body was one hundred fifty percent positive this man was exactly what she needed.

"We should go," he said in a husky voice as if he knew what she was thinking, and his mind was full of the same decadent images of them together.

"Yes," she said. His nostrils flared at her whispered response.

He frowned and put a hand on her lower back to guide her out of the building to the car waiting for them. Inside the car he left a disappointingly safe distance between them. He cleared his throat. "I booked an outside table at Bayside Catch. I took a chance you like seafood."

"I do." *I'd eat it even if I didn't.* "I'm not a picky eater. Never have been. Put it on a plate and I'll devour it. I should be two hundred pounds, but I burn it off with nerves I guess." *Shut up. Women probably throw themselves at him constantly. I'm sure they don't brag about cleaning their plates when they do.*

He gave her a funny look then smiled. "A man could be tempted to test that claim."

How Kenzi felt when she was with Dax overshadowed the dark thoughts usually circling within her. His presence was addictive. As he continued to watch her, she thought about what she'd said and her cheeks burned with a blush. "I didn't mean it that way."

I'm blushing like I'm innocent because I feel innocent with him.

I could convince myself the past never happened if it meant I could stay here, in this moment, continuing to feel this damn good.

"What way?" he asked.

She tried to read his expression. *What does he see when he looks at me? Does he know?* "Oh, I'm sorry. I thought you were . . ." Her voice trailed away when he took her hand in his.

"Flirting? I was."

"Oh." It was all she said because she was having trouble thinking about anything past how good her hand felt in his.

His eyes dropped to her lips, and for a moment she thought he might kiss her, but instead he gave her hand a squeeze and turned his gaze forward. "You chose the right dress."

"Lexi did, actually." Kenzi kicked herself for blurting out the truth. "What I mean is—" The lie died on her lips when her eyes met his again.

The lines of his face were harshly set. "I have a reputation for being brutally honest. Some say it's a flaw, but my friends value it. I have no time or patience for anything but the truth."

Kenzi's hand went cold in his. People said that, but they never meant it. She thought of the times she'd tried to speak to her family honestly and how much she'd lost because of it. The years she'd spent away from her family both for high school and college had felt like a punishment at first and then a sort of reprieve. At least when she was away from them she didn't have to lie. "Sometimes the truth is ugly."

His hand tightened on hers. "More often than not."

It was an oddly deep conversation to have with a man she knew next to nothing about. He didn't know her, either. Was that part of what made it tempting to be herself?

She gave herself a mental shake. *Can't I just enjoy a night out with a gorgeous man? Do I have to overthink the life out of it? He wants honesty; well, let's see how he handles it.* "I usually dress conservatively, but my friend had a dress that could do exactly what you asked for. Was she right?"

His hand tightened on hers again and when his eyes met hers she saw desire there. "Oh, yes."

Forget about everything else. Find the good. Cling to it. Kenzi bit back a smile. Basking in his gaze, she felt sexy and younger than she had in a long time. "I'm glad," she said cheekily.

His nostrils flared. "You're playing with fire, Kenzi."

She laced her fingers with his and leaned against his arm. "My life could use some heat."

His indrawn breath was swift and audible. "I don't believe in relationships. This would be one night, Kenzi. I'm flying to London tomorrow, and I have no intention of returning."

Kenzi fought back disappointment. That was the catch. There was always a catch. He wanted one night. At least he was honest. She searched his face. He didn't look like a player, spouting lines he hoped would get her into his bed. He was acknowledging the attraction between them and leaving no doubt as to whether or not he'd call the next day. There was something reassuring about that kind of honesty. "Did you come to Boston for me?"

"Yes."

Kenzi closed her eyes for a moment and let his answer wash over her. *Yes. He came for me.* She couldn't explain why, but she believed him. And she trusted him. If she asked him to end the date right then and drive her home, she believed he would.

One night.

No expectations of more than that.

There was a time when the answer would have been an easy yes. *But I'm not that person anymore. It didn't make anything better; it made me hate myself more.*

She opened her eyes and saw him watching her. She wished there was a way she could pause the date and call Willa and Lexi. She wasn't ready to say yes nor was she ready to say no. Honesty. He said he valued it. She licked her bottom lip and said, "Why don't we have dinner and see how it goes?" He nodded and looked forward again. An awkward silence dragged out despite the fact that they were still holding hands. When Kenzi could take it no more she joked, "I can handle the idea of no relationship, as long as dinner ends with dessert."

Desire burned in his eyes again. "It looks as though it will."

"I didn't mean—" Kenzi started to say, then she smiled wryly. "Maybe I did."

A chuckle rumbled in his chest. "You're different than I remember, Kenzi Barrington."

"In a good way?"

"In a million wonderfully surprising ways."

A tear spilled at his words because Kenzi knew he meant it. "You're less blurry." Kenzi fought an impulse to throw herself into his arms and declare dinner unnecessary. She didn't, though. No matter how their date ended, there was not a single thing she wanted to rush about this night.

They stayed on safe topics for the remaining drive to the restaurant. They compared favorite local restaurants and found they had similar tastes. They both preferred traditional foods over trendy creative cuisine.

"A good steak doesn't need a pineapple or some sauce no one can pronounce," he said with authority.

"Nor should it be the size of a credit card," she added, amazed at how easy he was to talk to. "Want to see me happy? Give me prime rib as big as my head and don't judge me when I finish every last bite."

He laughed. "It's a shame I chose a seafood restaurant. I'd like to see that."

"Shame you don't believe in second dates or you could." His hand tensed on hers, and Kenzi regretted letting herself banter so freely with him. *I'm going to ruin this date before it has a chance to really begin.* She shot him a quick look to gauge his expression and found him watching her. A quick apology was on the tip of her tongue, but she didn't voice it. He said he valued honesty. *I won't apologize for who I am or what I think. I do that too much already.* She held his gaze in a silent standoff. *Take it or leave it. This is the real me.*

He raised his hand to caress one of her cheeks. "You make me wish I were a different kind of man."

"Funny, you make me want to be myself."

His eyes lit with pleasure at her words, and he ran his thumb lightly across her lips. "I'm not what you need."

"Then why does this feel so good?" Kenzi asked in a whisper. It did feel good. All she could think about was his touch and the need it created within her.

He leaned closer, and his lips hovered above hers. His breath teased and warmed. So close. "Are you sure you're okay with one night?"

Maybe it was his deep, bedroom voice or the way his eyes never left hers, but Kenzi was mesmerized. There was no embarrassment. No coy flirtation. They were two people connecting on a primal, sexual level. Her chest rose and fell with the ragged breaths she was taking. "Got it. One night. No tomorrow. No promises. No prime rib."

He frowned at her final words and sat back, breaking the spell. Kenzi looked out the window and put her hands on her warm cheeks. *He's not happy and it's little wonder. He's wondering what he's doing on a date with a woman who is an emotional train wreck. And he knows it. Somehow, even though I've tried to conceal it, he knows.*

Kenzi glanced at him then looked away again. He didn't look happy and a memory of the night she'd met him came flooding back. He might seem open because of his honesty, but she had the feeling he didn't let anyone in.

Can I sleep with a man I know feels nothing for me?

And why isn't the answer to that question a simple no?

Thankfully, arriving at the restaurant gave Kenzi a reprieve from talking. A hostess led her and Dax through a dining room to a deck overlooking the ocean where there was one lone table. Heaters flanked an area where the table had been set up with a white tablecloth and candles.

Once seated, the hostess handed them menus and said, "It's usually so loud out here you can't hear the waves, but you'll be able to tonight. When my boyfriend proposes, I hope he does something like this. You must be celebrating something very special."

"It's our first date," Kenzi supplied, watching Dax's expression for a reaction, but he gave nothing away.

The hostess clapped her hands and beamed. "That is so romantic. I hope when I'm your age I'm still doing things like that. I'll probably be married with a ton of kids by then, though."

She walked off and Kenzi and Dax burst out laughing at the same time. Kenzi said, "She just called us old."

"What is she, twelve?"

"Eighteen probably. Apparently twenty-eight looks ancient to her."

"Then I shouldn't tell her I'm thirty-four or she'll offer me a walker."

"Thirty-four? Wow, you *are* old."

Dax threw his napkin at her. "I'll show you old."

Kenzi threw the napkin back. "Easy, Tiger, don't do anything to throw out your back. At your age, you have to be careful."

They shared another laugh then Dax's expression turned serious. Kenzi wanted to ask him what he was thinking but didn't. She wasn't that brave yet. Instead she turned her attention to the menu, and he followed suit. After they had ordered their drinks and food, Dax said, "You didn't want wine?"

"I don't normally drink."

He nodded. "You said that."

"But you weren't sure."

"People often say whatever they think I want to hear. Your honesty is refreshing."

Kenzi met his eyes. *Is this a test?* "Before you hand me a trophy, I lie like a rug when I'm cornered. I've pretty much turned lying into a lifestyle."

"That doesn't sound like you."

"Only because you don't know me." *This is me. Not perfect, but finally honest with someone.*

He sat back in his chair and folded his arms across his chest as if he were trying to solve a puzzle. "You're quite the enigma. Most women try to impress me."

Kenzi rolled her eyes. "Can you hear yourself when you speak because I'm not sure you'd say half of what you do if you could."

He laughed. "See, that's what I mean. You say whatever you're thinking. I like that."

With you. Only with you. There was a comfort to their exchange that was as pleasurable as their attraction to each other. "I don't have to worry what you think of me. You already said I won't see you again after tonight."

He frowned. "I did." He gave her a funny look. "A woman like you should demand better than that."

A memory from the past nipped at Kenzi and brought an edge to her next words. "You have no idea what kind of woman I am."

"So tell me," he said softly.

Kenzi panicked and gave him the same smile she often hid behind with her family. "There's nothing to tell."

"You said you didn't have to lie to me because I don't matter." He lowered his arms, leaned forward, and pinned her to her chair with those intense eyes of his.

Those beguiling eyes. "If it sounded that way, I'm sorry. That's not what I meant."

"Don't be sorry, be honest."

"I'm not ready to be," she said huskily, looking anywhere but at Dax.

"Then tell me," he said in a tone so gentle Kenzi almost burst into tears.

Kenzi took a deep, shaky breath and met his eyes again. "Can we rewind and forget this conversation happened? I don't want to be me tonight, Dax. I want to be on a fun date. I want to laugh, have a great meal, and see where all this goes. And if I never hear from you again, I'll make myself be okay with it because that's what I do, Dax. I'm a survivor."

Dax took her hand in his again. She wasn't sure if he would end the night or rush them back to her apartment before she changed her mind. She didn't expect him to lace his fingers with hers and say, "So am I, Kenzi. So am I." Then he cleared his throat and called the waitress over. He turned away to say something to the waitress without Kenzi being able to hear. The waitress looked surprised at first, but he handed her several bills and then she looked thrilled.

Once they were alone again, Kenzi couldn't help but ask, "What did you say to her?"

He looked as if he debated telling her, then he said, "I told her to cancel your order of salmon and bring you a prime rib the size of your head."

Kenzi shook her head as she digested that. "Prime rib wasn't on the menu."

He sat back and looked pleased with himself. "They serve it at Ranch House Grill around the corner."

"You sent her to get food from another restaurant? Can you do that?"

"You know as well as I do that anything is possible if you throw enough money at it. The owner understands that I'll compensate him well if he makes this evening perfect."

Kenzi searched Dax's face for a clue of what it meant. "I don't understand."

"I DON'T EITHER, but I want to see where this goes." Dax was as surprised by his words as Kenzi was. He could barely recognize himself. She obviously was open to sleeping with him, and he was definitely interested in sleeping with her. The outcome should be simple, but nothing was simple when it came to Kenzi. His emotions were jumbled together, making it difficult to think clearly, and the hard-on he'd been sporting all evening wasn't helping.

He wanted to cancel the meal and drag her off to the nearest bed.

He wanted to hug her until she trusted him enough to tell him whatever she felt she needed to hide. Had someone abused her? Had she done something she was ashamed of? He fought back a desire to shake her and promise her nothing would change how he felt about her.

What the fuck is wrong with me?

He'd told her to expect to never hear from him again. It was a talk he'd given women in the past, and he'd meant it when he'd said it.

I'm angry with her for accepting that shit?

Angry with myself because I'd never see her eat prime rib?

He shook his head and realized how he felt had nothing to do with watching her eat her favorite meal. *I don't want this to be the last time I see her.*

Conversation became strained while he tried to unravel the clusterfuck of his thoughts. In an apparent attempt to lighten the mood, she asked him if he'd always lived in London. He didn't normally talk much about himself, but she was interested, and soon he was describing his college days in Boston and how he'd once thought he would live there, but had ultimately chosen London because he was more comfortable there. He hadn't realized until he said it, but London hadn't been solely a business decision. "My mother was English so I have dual citizenship. I went to boarding school in the UK, but finished high school in the United States after my father died."

"I'm so sorry to hear that. Your father was American?"

"Yes, as was the uncle who raised me after he passed."

"I'm surprised you didn't move in with your mother."

"I don't know her."

"You don't know your mother?" Kenzi exclaimed then lowered her voice. "I'm sorry. It's none of my business."

Normally that's exactly what Dax would have said. His past was no one's business but his. Yet, there he was, leaning forward again, and ready to tell her anything she wanted to know. "My mother left my father when I was very young. I don't remember her. My guess is that my father paid her to stay away. I don't really know nor have I ever cared enough to look into it. When she left me, she ceased to matter."

Kenzi gave his hand a tight squeeze. "If she chose money over you, Dax, she cheated herself out in the end. Does she stay in touch with any of your family?"

"I don't have any family. My father and uncle were it." Dax hated the sympathy he saw in Kenzi's eyes and how desperately he wanted to kiss her just then. He pulled his hand away from hers.

She studied his expression for a long moment then asked, "Who are you more like—your father or your uncle?"

He almost ended the conversation there but didn't. He sensed she needed to see that he had his own scars. And if it made her less ashamed of her own, he would let her examine every last one of his. "I wish I could say neither, but I'm more likely the composite of the worst of both of them. My father was weak and lacked integrity and loyalty. My uncle was brutal and had no patience for weakness. I've made a good living on the financial misfortune of others, and I don't regret a single take-over, not even when I knew the owners. I guess you could say I'm genetically predisposed to be an asshole."

"I don't think you're an asshole," she said softly.

"Give me time," he said, half joking, half serious.

Kenzi smiled but it didn't reach her eyes. She looked as confused as he felt. He asked her about where she'd gone to school, and she vaguely described attending a high school and college in Canada. He wanted to ask her why she'd gone to school so far away from her family when their meals arrived.

She toyed with her prime rib, cutting it but not taking a bite. He pushed his food around his plate without tasting it either. "Do you want to get out of here?" he asked.

"Yes," she said then looked down at her plate apologetically. "I'm sorry. Normally I would scarf this down, but my stomach is doing nervous flips."

"I'm not hungry either," he said and motioned to the waitress. She cleared the still full plates away and asked if they wanted it wrapped up. Neither of them answered her at first. He was waiting for her to say something, give him a hint of what she was feeling. She met his eyes briefly then told the waitress she didn't think so.

Does her refusal include what had been on the menu after the restaurant? If so, it's for the best. I already want to toss her over my shoulder and haul her back to London with me like some bounty I've claimed as my own. I thought seeing her again would lessen the fascination I have with her. That plan failed. If I fuck her, I don't know if I can walk away.

I'd stay the night. Clay was right—seeing her was a bad idea.

She doesn't need a man like me.

She needs someone who'd protect her, cherish her.

A battle raged within him for a good part of the drive back to her apartment. During the drive, she turned away from him and looked as if she wanted to be anywhere but beside him. He couldn't blame her. He'd taken many women to dinner, more than he cared to admit, and he couldn't remember any of those evenings ending on the strained note this one had.

He reached out and took her hand in his, saying words that weren't normally in his vocabulary. "I'm sorry." *Sorry I can't be the man you need.*

Her eyes flew to his, and she gave him a sad smile. "No, I'm sorry. I haven't been myself lately. You came all this way to take me out. I don't know how I was when I was drunk, but I'm sure you're disappointed with the reality of who I am."

She believes that.

He pulled her against his chest and gave her the hug she looked as if she needed. She settled against him with a heartfelt sigh. The desire to kiss her lost against the decision he'd made. Even if it meant not having her, he would never hurt her. She was worth more than a one-night stand. "Disappointed is far from how I'm feeling."

She turned her head so she could see his face. He could tell she wanted to ask him what he was feeling, but she didn't. She just kept looking at him with those big eyes of hers that somehow made his heart beat double time.

His gaze fell to her lips, but he pulled them back to her eyes. "I've never wanted to kiss anyone as much as I want to kiss you right now. I want to haul you onto my lap and take you right here, right now, and lose myself in you. I don't care who sees. I want to wrap those gorgeous legs around my ass and fuck you until neither of us can remember our names."

Her hand fisted. "But? But what? What kind of sick game are you playing?"

He released her. "I'm not playing, but you're right, I'm

not staying."

Desire and disappointment burned in her eyes. She crossed her arms in front of her, an act that widened the cleavage of her dress—a fact he would have told her if the view weren't so tantalizing.

The car pulled up to the front of her apartment, and the driver discretely allowed Dax the privacy of opening the door himself and helping Kenzi out. They stood on the darkened sidewalk staring at each other until Kenzi said, "Well, thank you for dinner."

Dax was tempted to say, "You mean thanks for being the reason you couldn't eat your favorite meal?" but didn't. He mirrored her polite tone instead. "Thank you for going out with me."

Kenzi took out her key and turned away then turned back and glared at him. She wanted to say something to him; that much was obvious.

Her frustration with him mirrored his own. The idea brought a wry smile to his face. "Good night, Kenzi."

She shook her head. "That's it? If this is how you are I can see why a second date isn't necessary."

His eyes narrowed and his smile left. *I'm being fucking nice for once, and she's goading me. Why?*

She waved a hand in his direction. "I should have known you were all talk."

He didn't like what he assumed was her motivation. He closed the distance between them and pulled her against him, against his swollen cock. "What are you testing? Do you think if you push me I'll take what I want? I won't.

Some things should never be stolen and kisses are one of them. It's not that I don't want you, I do, but you're better than this. If I took what you're offering, I'd hate myself for it. And I have a feeling you'd hate me, too. Whoever hurt you, Kenzi, made you feel like you're not in control of what happens to you. You think you don't deserve to be treated well. You do and you always should be. Stop trying to get me to hurt you. I won't."

"No one—" Kenzi stopped herself from saying more. Tears filled her eyes. "Please leave now."

He let her go. "Kenzi—"

She turned away. "I'm fine."

They both knew she was lying, but this time he didn't call her on it. He let her walk away and told himself the night had ended the only way it could have. He stayed until she was safely in her building, until after he'd spoken to her bodyguard and knew she was being watched over. Only then did he force himself to leave.

Chapter Six

KENZI WASN'T REALLY proud of herself for avoiding her phone for the next two days, even when Lexi and Willa called. She didn't want to talk to anyone, especially if it involved trying to explain a date she had rehashed in her head about a hundred times and still couldn't figure out.

She'd spent so many hours thinking about what Dax had said. Had she really wanted to push him into losing control? Why would she want him to become just another man she slept with?

Because then he wouldn't matter?

And what did it mean that he'd refused her?

She remembered the evidence of his desire pressing against her. He said he was predisposed to being an asshole, but when she'd needed him to be he'd been gentle and supportive.

If he's attracted to me, why did he leave without even kissing me?

Because I'm worth more than the one night he offered?

Was that a compliment—or bullshit to end a date that had gone south?

The intercom on the wall near her door buzzed. Kenzi looked at the clock on the wall then at her flowered pajamas and groaned. Which one of her brothers had been given the assignment of bringing her back to the fold? She trudged over and hit the button and said, "Please tell Mom and Dad you couldn't find me."

"Open the door, Kenzi," her father said in a tone that reminded her of how he used to talk to her when she was much younger.

Kenzi laid her forehead against the wall above the intercom and closed her eyes. *Shit.* "Dad, I'm sorry. I just couldn't handle Mom today."

There was a heavy moment of silence, then he said, "She's beside me."

Double shit.

Resigning herself to the drama about to unfold, Kenzi pressed the button to open the door below. She sent Parker a quick text to inform him they were on their way up. She fixed her hair the best she could then practiced a bright smile in the mirror. She was still smiling when the elevator opened and her parents exited.

Sophie rushed forward, "Are you unwell, Kenzi? You should have called us. Dale, doesn't she look pale?" She put her hand on Kenzi's forehead. "You don't have a fever."

Kenzi backed away and led them into her apartment. "I'm fine, Mom."

"You don't look fine," Sophie said in a worried voice. "We've been calling all day." She lowered her voice. "Is it a female issue you don't want to discuss in front of your father?"

Kenzi sat on the couch instead of answering. She pulled her legs up in front of her and hugged them. "No, Mom. It's not that."

"Dale, it's the afternoon and she's still in her pajamas. Something is obviously wrong."

Her father sat across from Kenzi, his face creased with concern. "Kenzi, whatever it is, you need to snap out of it. You're upsetting your mother—"

Kenzi couldn't keep a defensive edge out of her voice. "For once, could this not be about Mom?"

Sophie gasped and sat beside Dale.

Dale put his hand on his wife's leg in support and said in a stern voice, "Kenzi—"

Kenzi closed her eyes and shook her head. She felt cornered. Normally she would have kept calm, kept her thoughts to herself, but everything building inside her lately came to a head at that moment. Her eyes flew open and she snapped, "I don't want my birthday to be in March anymore. My birthday is in April. Fucking April."

Sophie's eyes rounded. "Did you take a pill? Are you on something?"

Kenzi stood. "No, I'm not on something. I'm tired of pretending to be happy when I'm not."

Sophie looked to her husband and then back at her daughter. "This is why you won't take our calls? We've always celebrated your birthday in March. Ever since you were a baby. It never bothered you before."

"It has always upset me. But you don't know that because I've never told you. That's the point. I can't remember ever having a real birthday party. I should have had one. I should have told you I wanted one."

Sophie searched Kenzi's face. "Are you saying you want a party?"

Kenzi threw her hands up in frustration. "No, this isn't about a party. It's about me and all the things I've been too afraid to tell you. I can't keep it all in anymore. You need to know how I feel. I'm so angry with you about so many things. I hate that you sent me away. Why couldn't you listen to what I wanted? Why couldn't we fight about it like normal families do? You packed me up and sent me away. Just because you didn't approve of my friends?"

"It wasn't just your friends. We couldn't let you date Dean Henderson. We love him, but after he was arrested you had to understand why we didn't want him around you."

"I was never going to date Dean, and he wasn't the problem," Kenzi snarled. In the face of Kenzi's anger, Sophie began to shake with emotion. Kenzi had never spoken to her mother this way before, but she couldn't stop. It was as if a pressure valve had popped off, and what she'd held back for so long was too much to contain. She wouldn't have brought her anger to their door, but she was in her own home, already retreating as much as she was willing to. Like a cornered animal, she lashed out. "I tried to tell you that back then, but you didn't believe me. Or you didn't care how I felt. I don't know. I wasn't allowed to talk about it. We've never been allowed to talk about anything that matters because everyone is so afraid to upset you that we all suffer in silence."

"That's enough, Kenzi," her father warned. He stood, placing himself between Kenzi and Sophie. "I won't have you speaking to your mother this way."

"Then you'd better leave, because I haven't even begun to share what I'm holding in."

Sophie stood next to Dale. "What happened? This isn't our Kenzi."

Kenzi hugged her arms around herself. "Yes, it is. The real me. I don't want to be in Boston. I don't want to be pressured to visit you. Game night is a joke. The only reason we go is the same reason we do anything, Mom, because it's what *you* want. Bad things happen to everyone, but you've let one tragedy rule all of our lives. I'm sorry my twin died. I'm sorry you went through that, but do we all have to pay the price because you blame yourself for something that would have probably happened even if you hadn't been out of the country? It wasn't your fault, but it wasn't mine, either. I love you, Mom, but I won't feed into your fantasy that we're one big happy family anymore. Because we're not. We never have been. I'm just the only one with the courage to tell you."

Tears began pouring down Sophie's face. She was pale when she turned slowly and walked out the door.

Dale turned on his daughter, angrier than she'd ever seen him. "If your goal was to hurt your mother tonight, you succeeded. I hope you're proud of yourself."

Only after the door had slammed behind her father did Kenzi sink into the couch and cover her face with her hands.

She replayed the scene with her parents in her head, and each time she felt worse. All of it was true, but she regretted how she'd said it. On impulse, she picked up the note Dax had sent her.

Am I? Am I stronger than what I'm facing? It doesn't feel that way.

She picked up her phone. Dax's number was still in the phone history. Calling him made no sense. She hadn't heard from him since their date. He was probably back in London. Probably already with another woman.

None of that stopped her from choosing his number. It rang once and she almost hung up. He picked up on the second ring, "Marshall."

"Dax? It's Kenzi."

KENZI?

What the fuck?

Still in Boston, fresh from a heated call from Dean Henderson, Dax's adrenaline was pumping. That little shit had the balls to warn him to back off Poly-Shyn.

Dax had almost told Dean he'd already lost interest in the venture, but Dean kept the threats coming until Dax lost his temper. "Be very careful, Dean."

"You be careful. Go back to London. Stay away from Poly-Shyn and Kenzi Barrington."

"What does Poly-Shyn have to do with Kenzi?"

"Nothing, but I know you took her to dinner. I know your reputation, and the last thing she needs is someone like you messing with her. Stay the fuck away from her."

"Or what?" Dax asked the question even though all sense told him not to.

"You'd be wise not to stick around to find out. If you're looking for a fight, I'll bring it every time, and I always win." Dean had hung up before Dax had the chance to bring it right then.

See, this is why people need to learn to shut the fuck up. Now I have to acquire Poly-Shyn just to teach that little shit a lesson. He called his team in for a meeting and ordered them to start buying Poly-Shyn shares as soon as the market opened in the morning. It was a classic English maneuver to strike without warning before the company had time to have their first meeting of the day, but it was effective. His team was experienced with his methods. They knew how much to buy, the contacts necessary within the company, and what to release to the press. As usual, his team would handle the paperwork side; he'd handle the fallout.

He was still pondering how Dean had known about Kenzi and what their relationship was when she called.

"Is this a bad time?" she asked. The hitch in her voice told him it was for her.

He took a deep breath and ran a hand through his hair in frustration. "It's not the best."

"Sorry," she said, "I shouldn't have called. It's probably late where you are."

He swore and sat down at his desk, hating how abrupt he'd been with her. "I'm still in Boston. Don't hang up. What did you want, Kenzi?"

The line was silent for a long moment, then she said,

"The truth?"

"Always."

"I needed to hear your voice."

Her answer knocked the breath clear out of him. He'd spent the last two days telling himself she'd be better off if he stayed away from her. He hadn't gone as far as to fly back to London, but he'd almost convinced himself that staying had nothing to do with her. Now there she was, telling him she *needed* him? It was enough to nearly kill a man who was trying not to take advantage of the situation. "Did something happen?"

"Yes."

His conversation with Dean was quickly forgotten in the face of Kenzi's distress. He sat straighter in his chair, already angry with whoever had hurt her.

"I hurt someone I love very much," she added sadly. "I said things I shouldn't have. I didn't mean to. It's just that once I started speaking everything gushed out. How do I say sorry when what I said was true?"

Dax couldn't remember the last time someone had turned to him with a problem that wasn't business related. He wasn't sure where to begin. "Who did you hurt?"

"My parents." She paused. "You don't want to hear this."

"I do." Dax opened his office door and motioned to his secretary to hold his calls. He closed the door and sat in the chair in front of his desk. He wasn't proud of the relief that flooded through him when she said it wasn't a lover or old boyfriend. "Are you close to your parents?"

"Yes and no. We try to be. It's a long story."

With anyone else that would have been Dax's cue to exit the conversation, but he wanted to know everything about her. "Stop hedging and just tell me, Kenzi. I'm here and I'm listening." The sound of her sobbing filled him with a rush of emotions he wasn't used to. He wanted to hang up and run from her—or to her. She tangled him up in a way he had no defense against. "Don't cry. Whatever is wrong it can be fixed."

She sniffed loudly. "Some things can't be, but I'm not crying over that." He wasn't used to feeling lost, but he had no idea what she was talking about or what she expected from him. All he knew was he wanted to be there for her. She blew her nose loudly. "I wasn't sure if I should call you, but you hear me. You really do. I feel like I can be myself with you, and you can handle it."

A warm feeling spread through Dax. "I can. So tell me what it is you're holding back."

"I don't know if I can."

Dax's chest tightened, and he leaned forward in the seat. He had a feeling he knew what she was going to say. Part of him didn't want it to be true, but wanting things to be different never changed anything. Ugly reality was best faced head-on. "Whatever it is, it won't change the way I see you, nor will it go farther than me."

"I'm a big lie, Dax. A big fat lie. My family doesn't know. My friends don't know. And it's eating me up on the inside."

"Then let it out. I'm here, Kenzi. Right here."

After a pause she started talking in a calmer tone. "You

have to understand; my family doesn't handle things well. They either don't react or they overreact. I had a twin. We never talk about him. He died at birth. My mother has never been right since. She had a breakdown when I was an infant, and my family has lived in fear of it happening again for . . . twenty-eight years. We don't talk about it, but it's always there. Looming as a possibility. We grew up knowing we had to be careful not to upset her. We had to be perfect in front of her. And I was. At least I tried to be. I kept my questions to myself. I pretended along with everyone else that every year we weren't gathering for a week to mourn the loss of a brother none of us ever knew. I know my parents love me, but when I needed them the most they sent me away. Part of me hates them for it."

"Why did you need them, Kenzi? What happened?"

"It shouldn't affect me anymore. It was thirteen years ago."

Dax's hand clenched on the phone. "I'm coming over."

"No. I couldn't say this to your face."

Dax forced himself to stay seated. "Okay."

"I was stupid, Dax. I snuck out to a party I shouldn't have. Dean warned me to stay away from the guy, but I thought I was a better judge of people."

"What guy?"

"I can't say, Dax. I don't ever want to say or hear his name. Can you understand that?"

"Yes." *Although that won't save him. Nothing will stop me from finding him.*

After a quiet moment, Kenzi continued, "I chose to leave

the party with him. I chose to drink the alcohol he gave me. What happened was my fault, I know that, but it wasn't right."

"What did he do?" *Because pain will soon be coming his way.*

She let out an emotional breath. "Exactly what you think. I tried to say no, but nothing I said mattered. When it was over he dropped me back at the party like it hadn't happened. But it had. The next day Dean beat the guy so badly he almost killed him. I don't know how he found out because no one else ever did. Suddenly the police were asking questions about Dean. I was scared. Scared of how my mother would react. Scared of what people would think of me. I just kept quiet, and the longer I kept quiet the more I couldn't say anything. I eventually tried to tell my parents, but I didn't get past the part where I'd snuck away to the party. They were already so angry that the truth didn't matter. They believed Dean was a bad influence on me and sent me to a boarding school."

"Kenzi, what that bastard did was not your fault."

"Maybe not, but everything since has been. I should have stood up for Dean instead of getting him in trouble for defending me. I'm not the perfect daughter my parents think they raised. I'm not the innocent I pretend to be. I went into a bad place for a while when I first went away. I did drugs. I went from one bad relationship to another. I tried everything to wipe it away, to look myself in the mirror and not be ashamed of who I was. But nothing wipes it away. I thought I could put it behind me, just pretend none of it ever happened. It worked for a while, but lately I can't get it out of my head. I'm twenty-eight years old, and I am not the person I thought I would be. Do you know what I do with my time? Nothing. Do you know what I care about? Nothing. I'm going to turn thirty before I know it, and I haven't done a single thing that matters. All I've done is lie to myself and others. I don't want to live like that anymore, but I don't know what to do next."

I hope that bastard is still alive because I'm going to kill him.

Kenzi let out a half-laugh, half-sob. "I told you I'm a mess. My brothers do whatever the hell they want. They took what happened to us and they used it as motivation to succeed in the business world. Me? I shut down instead. I waste my time dreaming about how I wish things were. Do you know why I love islands? I listen to the sound of the waves, and I imagine what my life would have been like if my brother had lived, how everything might have been different. I have this reoccurring fantasy of us all being together and happy. I know it can't happen, but when I go to an island I feel closer to a brother I never met. So that's it, that's how I've been doing. Not too well." She blew her nose again. She was silent for a few minutes then said, "Thank you for letting me finally say this to someone."

"Shit, Kenzi." There was so much he wanted to say that he couldn't find the words to articulate. "Is this what you told your parents?"

She laughed without humor. "Thankfully, no. It was bad enough when I told them I hate never celebrating my birthday because it would upset my mother. I may have mentioned how I don't like game night and that I was sick of pretending to be happy when I'm not. It was enough to send my mother running and earn me a lecture from my father. They can't handle the truth." She sighed. "I completely understand if you never want to hear from me again, but you don't know how good it felt to finally say it out loud."

Dax rubbed a hand harshly across his face. "Where are you?"

"My apartment," she answered tentatively.

"I'll be there in thirty minutes."

"No. Wait," she said in a rush. "You can't come here."

Dax stood. "Give me a good reason why I can't."

"After everything I said . . ."

"Wear comfortable shoes. It's beautiful outside. I'm taking you for a walk in the sunshine."

"Please don't feel that you have to—"

Dax was already texting his driver to meet him downstairs. "Kenzi, I don't do a damn thing I don't want to do. I need some fresh air and you do, too. Unless you don't want to see me. If not, say it now."

Kenzi made a soft sound that might have been from crying again. "I'll be ready when you get here."

Before he hung up, Dax said, "Kenzi, you are a beautiful woman—inside and out. Knowing what that bastard did doesn't change how I feel. I'll see you in a few minutes."

"Yes," she said as if she wasn't sure it was really happening.

Dax shot off an email to his team telling them to hold off

on his earlier instructions then strode out of his office and made it out of the building in record time. On the drive to her apartment he admitted to himself that he hadn't been honest with her. What she'd said had shaken him. He kept his distance from people. He told himself they were all replaceable.

But Kenzi.

Well, she'd just found a way into his heart.

And he had a feeling nothing would ever be the same.

Chapter Seven

KENZI RUSHED THROUGH showering, doing her hair, and applying makeup. She briefly hesitated while choosing what to wear then decided on simple slacks and a blouse. Dax wasn't on his way over to take her on their second date. He was checking in on her because she'd called him like a support hotline.

She gave herself one last look in the mirror. Her eyes were red from crying, but there was a spark of hope in them that hadn't been there for a long time. *I told him. I told him everything. And he didn't run from me. He didn't shatter beneath the weight of it.*

Her eyes misted up, but she dabbed the tears away before they could ruin her makeup. *Reality, I know you have to come crashing in soon, but please don't let it be today. Let me have one day where I am with someone who sees the real me and still thinks I'm not broken.*

She waited on the outside steps of her apartment building. Dax was right, being in the sunshine was just what she needed. She took several deep breaths. It was hard not to run to meet him when his car pulled up. She stayed where she was, though, and waited.

The look in his eyes when he saw her almost had her crying again. She felt beautiful when he smiled at her that way. He stopped just before the bottom step and held his hand out to her. "Ready?"

She descended the stairs to join him. "You came."

He looked down at her with the oddest expression on his face. "Did you think I wouldn't?"

She searched his face. "I wouldn't have blamed you if you hadn't."

He cupped her face. "Kenzi, I will always come when you need me. Always." He turned, tucked her hand in his arm and drew her forward to walk with him down the busy sidewalk. It was a hefty promise from a man who hardly knew her, but Kenzi believed him. "Now, show me why you chose this neighborhood. Does it have anything to do with the bike path a block away?"

Kenzi smiled. He didn't feel like someone she'd just met. Their connection felt more real than anything she'd felt in a long time. "Yes. It runs along the river, and I love going there. It's peaceful but also always full of young people exercising or walking their dogs."

He guided her along. "I've never liked dogs."

She gave him a sidelong look. He was keeping to safe topics as if he knew she was still shaken from their earlier conversation. "Really? Why not?"

He shook his head. "They're messy and annoying. I don't see why people take animals that belong outside, bring them inside, then wonder why they destroy everything."

Did he honestly believe that? How sad. Then a thought came to her. "You've never had one."

"No."

In so many ways they were polar opposites. Dax spoke his mind and didn't back down. Kenzi had been raised to keep her thoughts to herself and put her feelings aside. Yet, somehow, they were alike. "I wanted a puppy when I was a child, but my father said a houseful of children was all my mother could handle. Pets were not an option."

Kenzi didn't expect Dax to say more on the topic, but for a moment he looked as if he were lost in the past. "Not for me, either. My father married and divorced three women before I was twelve years old, and none of them were my mother. I spent most of my time at boarding school, but when I was with my father we were always leaving for somewhere. I wasn't allowed to bring much with me. My father hated clutter. He only found value in the newest and shiniest of anything. He died in a plane crash with his fourth wife. The most important lesson he taught me was getting attached to anyone or anything is a waste of time and energy."

Kenzi stopped walking and pulled Dax to a halt beside her. "You don't believe that."

He frowned down at her. "I absolutely do."

She searched his face, and what she saw there wasn't the cold and bitter man he described. He was a man who had been hurt, maybe not in the same way she had been, but enough that he shut a part of himself down—just as she had. She'd bet her life on that. It was the softer side of him that drew her to him. "I'm getting attached to you. Is that a waste of time?"

"Don't look at me that way, Kenzi. I'm not the man you want to believe I am."

Kenzi shook her head. "You're not the man you think you are, either." She followed an urge and wrapped her arms around him, laying her head on his chest. Although being that close to him sent her senses into overload, her attraction to him came second to her desire to comfort him.

At first he held himself stiffly under control, then he gave in and pulled her tighter against him. She thought he would kiss her, but instead he buried his face in her hair. "God, Kenzi, I don't know what to do with you."

She waited for him to say more, explain what he meant, but he didn't.

He set her back from him and said, "Come on. Let's get something to eat."

When they exited the small coffee shop where they'd ordered drinks and sandwiches to go, the benches near it were taken, so they ate as they walked. A question had been brewing in Kenzi that she could no longer hold back. "When do you go back to London?"

He took a bite of his sandwich and chewed it slowly before answering. "I have a local project I need to resolve first."

Me? God, don't let that be how he sees me. Growing up with so many brothers had taught her that sometimes the depth she sought in a conversation simply wasn't there. There was a good chance when Dax described how he felt about a work venture, he was actually referring to work and nothing else. Still, the vague way he answered made her more curious. "What kind of project?"

"It's a complicated situation. I prefer to keep business just that—business. This one has the potential of becoming personal, and every time I think I have a clear handle on how to proceed, it takes another turn." He threw the rest of his sandwich in a trash barrel they passed and turned to her. "I don't want to talk business."

"Me either." The way he was looking at her made work the last thing on Kenzi's mind, too. There was a yearning in his eyes that echoed how she felt whenever she was near him. He stepped closer and bent his head until his mouth hovered just above hers. She licked her bottom lip. It would be so easy to close the distance between their mouths and kiss him. Their breath mingled. Kenzi had never wanted a man as much as she wanted him, and that she could feel that way without even touching him was as scary as it was exciting.

"You look better," he said huskily.

"Better?" she asked. Looking into his eyes, there was nothing before or after that moment. There was only him and how he made her feel.

"Than when I first came over. You're not blotchy anymore."

Kenzi blinked quickly a few times as his words sunk in. Her hands went to her hips and desire mixed with irritation. "My hearing must be off because it sounded like you just insulted me."

He chuckled. "Never." He ran one hand up the side of her neck and traced her chin. "You're beautiful in any color."

If his touch hadn't felt as good as it did, she might have still been offended. She tried to think of something witty to say to him, but all she could think about was the kiss he looked as if he were about to give her.

His phone buzzed in his pocket, and he swore. He checked his messages and Kenzi knew before he said it that he had to go. "I have an important meeting this afternoon I didn't think to cancel."

Kenzi pushed her disappointment aside and smiled. "That's okay. This was perfect. Thank you."

He replaced his phone in his pocket and offered her his arm. Their earlier walk had brought them disappointingly close to her apartment, and she was on her steps too soon.

"I'll call you," he said then turned away and disappeared into his town car.

Confused, Kenzi sat down on the steps and stayed there for a long time. Dax seemed to like her. There were times when she was convinced he was just as attracted to her as she was to him, but then he would pull away.

What did I expect his reaction would be when I told him the truth about me? I'm sure that's not a turn-on for many men. Still, he came because he was worried about me. So, he cares. Focus on that. There's the good. Everything else? Useless wishing. The only way my life will change is if I stop dreaming and start doing something.

Something worthwhile.

On the heels of that thought came the realization that she'd left her phone in her apartment. Messages from her family were probably waiting for her inside. She closed her eyes and turned her face toward the sun.

Everyone will want me to apologize. I'm not sorry about what I said, but I could have approached the conversation better. I can't go back to how things were before, but maybe I can find a way to be myself without hurting those I love.

I can do this.

Kenzi forced herself to leave the peace and quiet of outside. She checked her phone, but there were no missed calls. Nothing. Only because she found it impossible to sit still, she cleaned her apartment until it shone. Paid bills. Organized her closets. She did everything she could to keep her mind off her family and Dax.

She slept fitfully that night, remembering only snippets of the nightmares that had plagued her. After a quick shower and coffee, she called Willa. "Are you working today?"

"We were supposed to be, but it fell through. What do you need?"

Kenzi bolstered her courage and said, "I'm not happy with what I'm doing—or not doing as far as work right now. I need to come up with a plan. No one knows me as well as you and Lexi do. Could you help me? I want to make some major changes."

"Hang on." Willa called to her sister. "Lexi, get in the shower. We're heading over to Kenzi's place. She's decided to do something with her life and wants our input." *Ouch.* Leave it to softly spoken Willa to say it as it was. Her honesty was what Kenzi always loved, so it was impossible not to appreciate it in that moment, even if it stung a little.

"A full life makeover will cost her breakfast," Lexi replied. "Ask Kenzi if her cook can whip up those omelets we love."

Willa laughed, "Lexi wants to know. . ."

"On it," Kenzi said. Most of the time Kenzi cooked for herself, but she did have a cook on speed dial for special occasions. Willa said they'd be over soon and hung up. Kenzi exchanged a few quick texts with her cook, pocketed her cell phone, and smiled. Anyone else would have asked her a hundred questions or assured her that her life was fine as it was. Only Willa and Lexi knew her well enough to know she was serious. She trusted them as she trusted no one else.

Except Dax.

After how kind he had been the day before, she didn't really want to spill her problems all over him again. Still, she believed if she did, he would come by. *But I don't want him to be with me because he feels sorry for me.*

She shook her head and told herself to concentrate on things she could control. She could spend the night trying to figure out what Dax felt for her, but it wouldn't accomplish anything, and Kenzi was determined to start making better decisions.

The cook arrived and prepared decadently fattening breakfast then left just as Willa and Lexi appeared. All three of them ate more than they should have then moved over to the living room.

Willa brought a notebook and pen. Lexi carried her laptop in. Kenzi brought her courage. Although there were things she'd never told her friends, she wasn't afraid they'd judge her. They never had. Kenzi had spent quite a lot of time recently asking herself why she'd felt paralyzed emotionally. She could place the blame on how she'd been raised to keep a smile on her face and her thoughts to herself, but where she'd been didn't matter as much as where she was going.

"Before we start, I have something I need to tell you. Something I should have told you a long time ago, but I was afraid to." Kenzi took a deep breath and told her two closest friends about the night in high school that had changed her life. She shared her shame about Dean and how she'd held her silence even when he'd gotten in trouble with the law. They listened quietly as Kenzi concluded. "I know the reasons I am the way I am, but I want to be more. For a long time I have felt trapped inside myself. And I thought everyone was stopping me from being who I wanted to be. But I'm beginning to think I was stopping myself. I could have done things differently. I could do things differently now. I don't want to hurt anyone or disappoint my family, but I want to look in the mirror and like who I see. Can you help me figure out how to do that?"

Lexi and Willa exchanged a look.

Lexi said, "You told us all about it when we were in high school."

Mortified, Kenzi's mouth dropped open. "I did?"

Willa made a face and shrugged awkwardly. "It was when we first met you. You were wasted."

"You never said anything," Kenzi said slowly.

Lexi moved over to sit next to Kenzi. "We knew you didn't want to talk about it."

Willa sat on her other side. "We were so worried about you when we first met you, but then you seemed to put it behind you."

Lexi gave her shoulder a supportive pat. "But it's why we knew coming home would be hard for you."

Kenzi looked back and forth at her two friends. They'd attended college together so they could remain close, but she just realized they'd gone a step further for her. "So you came to Boston with me."

Lexi shrugged one shoulder. "We didn't have a lot tying us to Nova Scotia."

"And you're our family," Willa and Lexi said in unison. They exchanged another look and both said, "by choice."

"I love you two." Kenzi used a tissue to dab away a tear before it spilled forth.

"We love you, too," Lexi and Willa said together.

With a small smile, Kenzi said, "When you two get like this it's a little creepy."

"Like what?" they both asked, looked at each other, then laughed.

Willa pointed to her sister then herself. "The twin thing. Most of the time I look at Lexi and think we couldn't be more different, then when we get excited about something—"

"We sort of know what the other is thinking. It's weird," Lexi finished.

"I know," Kenzi said. She'd seen it happen many times over the span of their friendship, but their connection was always a little disconcerting. *Would I have had the same connection to my twin? Could we have read each other's minds?*

What ifs could drive me to distraction. Fascinating as it was to talk to them about being twins, it wasn't why Kenzi had asked them over. "Okay, so back to what I was saying. What are my options? I don't want an all-out family war. I don't want to hurt my mother, but I want to find my voice. I want to do something that makes up for what I didn't do. I don't know. Is it too late? Am I being ridiculous?"

Willa gave her a hug. "No, you're being the Kenzi we love. You're a good person, and you don't like to hurt anyone. That's why you never said anything. But what if talking about what happened to you could help someone? What if it could stop someone from putting themselves in dangerous situations?"

Lexi snapped her fingers in the air. "I know what you should do. Public speaking gigs pay really well. Remember the last one, Willa? *Three hundred dollars* and all we had to do was talk about dental floss at a conference. You could make money and help people."

Willa rolled her eyes. "Lexi, she doesn't need the money."

Lexi plopped back against the couch. "Oh, yeah." Then she sat forward as another idea hit her. "Do it for charity, then. Same thing, but better."

Kenzi nodded slowly as she considered it. "I have heard about speakers who go into high schools and help raise awareness on subjects like this. I never imagined myself as one of those people, though."

Willa hugged her. "You'd be perfect at it, Kenzi. Look at how long you've kept your silence because you've been afraid to say anything. Imagine if hearing you talk about what happened could help another woman face her own fears. Girls in high school need to hear that if they drink, they put themselves in danger. And if they decide to do it anyway, they need to watch out for each other. Or that when something does happen, no matter what they think, they can survive it. You could make a difference that way."

Kenzi held one hand of each of her friends and blinked back her tears. "Remember the idea I had for a reality show? I understand why I wanted it now. I was still too afraid to talk about what happened to me, and I thought everything would be better if it all came out—regardless of how. But I was wrong. This is my story, my message, and it's time for me to control it instead of the other way around. You're right, I can tell it my way. I refuse to be afraid anymore. Thank you."

Willa's eyes teared up as well. "Should I write this down?"

Kenzi chuckled. She felt stronger even though nothing had actually changed yet, nothing outside of her anyway. She could hear Dax's voice in her head telling her that she was in control of what happened to her and always would be. He'd been referring to sex, but Kenzi saw how little of a say she'd had in her life as a whole. She could accept that that's the way it was, or she could finally take a stand. "No, I've got this. I'll make a few calls. I bet there are organizations who do this and are in need of fundraising. I'm really good at that. I learned from the best." *My mom.* She rubbed her hands over her face. "Now for the million-dollar question—

do I tell my family now or after I've gone public?"

A FEW DAYS later Dax met Clay for an evening jog by the Charles River. Clay wasn't admitting to it, but Dax was reasonably certain he was sticking around Boston in case all hell broke loose. So far each time Clay had brought up Poly-Shyn or Kenzi, Dax had refused to comment on either. Their friendship had survived many years because they knew each other well enough to know when to push and when to wait for the other to work things out on his own.

When their jog wound down to a walk, Dax wiped the sweat from his face with one hand and took in a long, cleansing breath. "I told my team we're backing off Poly-Shyn."

Clay stretched as he walked. "That's a wise decision."

"It was exactly as you said: the fallout outweighed the potential profit."

"So it had nothing to do with that Barrington woman?"

"Why would it?"

"Oh, I don't know, maybe because you're sleeping with her."

"I'm not sleeping with her."

"Not yet?"

"Not yet. Not going to."

Clay shook his head in confusion. "Then what are you still doing in Boston?"

"I do have an office here and other projects I'm working on."

"That has never kept you stateside. Listen, you look like

shit. You completely dropped the ball on the island sale. I sent you two potential buyers, and you blew them off. I call your office and you're not there half the time. Are you in some kind of trouble?"

Dax stopped and watched a woman walk her dog onto the grass beside the path. She put down a small blanket, sat down on it, and called the dog over to sit on her lap. She took out a tablet and started reading something while petting her dog absently with her other hand. He pictured Kenzi in the woman's place and remembered the conversation they'd had about pets. Kenzi had grown up wealthy but also oddly deprived. In his experience women who were born into money as she had been were shallow creatures who cared more about what they were wearing than anything else. Kenzi was humble and grateful.

He thought about how she'd been raised, what had happened to her, and how the combination had shaped the beautiful woman she was. He hadn't called her for the same reason he hadn't kissed her, she was fragile and he wouldn't take advantage of that. She hadn't made that decision easy for him. There'd been times when she'd looked at him and he'd known he could have her in his bed if he wanted, but then what?

It was that last question that was new to him. Never before had he cared enough to ask—then what?

Every scenario he ran in his head concluded with her being hurt when it ended between them. And it would end. Everything did.

The only solution he'd come up with was to not give in

to the sexual attraction he had for her. If she called, he'd help her, but that's all. They couldn't be more.

"Dax?"

"Sorry." Dax's attention returned to the present. "I forgot your question."

Clay waved a finger at him. "That's my point. I've known you a long time, and I've never seen you like this. You can tell me it's none of my business, but what the hell is wrong with you?"

Dax looked back at the woman on the blanket. "If you wanted a dog, where would you get one?"

"A dog? Seriously?"

"Not for me."

"For Kenzi Barrington?"

"If she wants one, she deserves to have one."

"Oh, boy. Is Kenzi the reason you walked away from Poly-Shyn?"

"Yes. No. Fuck, it's complicated." Almost as complicated as tracking down the guy who had hurt Kenzi in high school only to discover he'd died in prison. From what Dax could uncover, the man had been convicted of stealing expensive cars from rich kids, but his ultimate punishment had come at the hands of a fellow inmate after bragging about liking young girls. Some crimes were too heinous for even a criminal to stomach. He ran a hand through his hair. "I'd like to see her happy, that's all."

"So she didn't ask you to back off the Henderson's company?"

"No, but Dean Henderson isn't as bad as I thought he

was. He'll lose the company anyway, but it won't be at my hands."

Clay turned and started jogging in place. "As fascinating as all of this is, I have a date tonight—with a woman I'm going to sleep with. That's the way it's supposed to work, Dax. You like a woman, you fuck her. You don't spare her old boyfriend's company, and you definitely don't buy her a puppy."

Dax fell into a jog beside Clay as they headed back the way they'd come. "She never dated Dean. I had a complete investigation done. They were friends. Nothing more."

Clay asked in a serious tone, "Promise me something?"

"What?"

"If I ever get like you are right now, beat the shit out of me."

Dax gave Clay a hearty shove. "I should do it now." He wasn't serious and they both knew it.

Clay's stumbled but laughed more and quickly righted himself. "Hey, be careful when choosing a dog for a woman you're falling for. Remember, those things live a while. You could end up with it at the end of your bed. Oh, wait, you have no intention of sleeping with her so that's fine."

"Shut the fuck up."

Chapter Eight

A WEEK LATER, Kenzi stepped out of her apartment in slacks, a blouse, and a blazer. Even though she was on her way to do something she normally would have found terrifying, she felt stronger than she had in a long time. She looked around the hallway and was pleased to see it empty. Although she'd hated doing it, she'd let Parker go. She'd given him a great reference and one of her friends had hired him almost instantly, so there was no guilt.

There was also no sign that her brothers had replaced him, likely because they didn't know he was gone. For the first time in her life, Kenzi's phone wasn't ringing with calls from her family. She'd gone to see her parents and apologized because it was what her parents expected. Her mother had asked questions, but Kenzi knew she wasn't ready to hear the answers. Or, rather, Kenzi wasn't ready for the fallout yet. She asked her parents to give her time to work out a few things on her own. Although her mother hadn't been happy when she'd left, they'd come to an understanding of sorts.

Kenzi could think clearer about what she wanted to do

once her family was, however temporarily, out of the equation. She contacted a not-for-profit organization that worked to bring speakers to high schools on a variety of social issues. After interviewing her, they thought she would be a perfect fit for their program. They helped her choose the best way to tell her story, light on the details, heavy on how she'd felt and how she'd survived it. Each time she told her story, she felt more empowered, freer. She was ready to share it now with an auditorium of students. At first she'd thought it would only be girls, but the program director had said that boys needed to hear her, too.

The news media hadn't been invited, which didn't mean the story wouldn't get out, but Kenzi was okay with whatever happened. Part of her thought she should have gone to her parents and told them what she was about to do, but this was for her, and they would have to understand that.

There was one person she wanted to tell. She'd wavered back and forth if she should. After all, she hadn't heard from him again. Still, she had something to say that went beyond the physical attraction between them. From the backseat of a taxi she called Dax.

"Kenzi."

"Do you have a minute?"

"Always." He made a sound like he was shuffling something around then said, "What's up?"

She blurted out that she was speaking at a high school about what had happened to her. She didn't give herself time to second-guess if she should be telling him. Instead she rushed to the reason she had called. "If I hadn't met you, I might not have found the courage to do this the right way. I was scared and I was angry, and that muddled my message. I felt out of control because I was out of control. Being honest with you allowed me to be honest with myself. You're probably praying for the day I stop calling you like this, but I had to tell you thank you. Nothing in my life has changed yet, but I have." After an awkward silence, Kenzi said, "So, thank you again."

Dax cleared his throat. "Kenzi, all I did was listen."

"Exactly," she said softly. "That's all I needed. Anyway, I'm sure you're busy, but I feel really good about what I'm doing today. Really good. And I thought you should know."

"Do you have anyone going with you?"

Kenzi clutched the phone. He would have gone if she'd asked him to. No matter what happened between them, it was impossible not to fall a little in love with him for that. "Two of my friends are going. Then they're taking me to lunch."

"Will you be home after that?"

"Yes."

"Good."

Kenzi expected him to say he wanted to see her or to ask her somewhere, but he didn't. She held her breath and waited.

"I'm in meetings most of the day, but if you need me, call."

Kenzi let out a shaky breath. "I'll be fine. Thanks, Dax." She hung up before she gave in to the impulse to ask him to come over. They were friends of a sort, and she told herself she'd find a way to be okay with that.

A few minutes later Kenzi was standing at a podium in front of a thousand high school students. The room was hushed as they waited for her to speak. Once she started speaking, once her story was out there, there would be no turning back. No more pretending. She remembered the director's advice to speak slowly and prayed she didn't hyperventilate. She started to introduce herself, stopped, and took a quick sip of water. Just then she met the eyes of a girl in the first row. She didn't look bored as some of the others did. She wasn't secretly texting or whispering something to her friends. She was looking at Kenzi with a kind of sad hopefulness Kenzi recognized. She told her story to that girl, and it flowed out of her more eloquently than she could have ever rehearsed it. She spoke of the shame and fear that had followed. She talked about how long she'd tried to keep it to herself, how she'd tried to convince herself it hadn't happened. How she'd thought for a long time that telling her story would hurt the people she loved, but what she'd discovered was she'd hurt them anyway because a secret like that slowly destroys a person. Her advice was to not wait in fear until you're almost thirty. You don't have to tell everyone; tell one person you trust.

Kenzi thought of Dax when she said that and her voice tightened with emotion. "One good person can change everything."

Kenzi met the eyes of the girl in the front as she finished her speech. The girl was wiping away tears. Kenzi hoped her message of hope and survival would give her the courage to share her own story, whatever that story was. When she listed off the confidential services that were available through the school, she prayed the girl found her way to one of them.

As Kenzi left the stage, there was a light applause, somewhat forced. Many of the students were already talking to their friends or texting. Kenzi didn't care. Her message had been heard by someone who needed to hear it. That was all that mattered.

When the director approached Kenzi and told her she'd done well, Kenzi took her aside and mentioned the girl in the front row. The director nodded sadly and said that she'd noticed her crying, also, and that she'd make sure she connected with a counselor. Kenzi knew well that there was no quick fix, no one thing anyone could say that would right whatever wrong had been done to the girl, but at least now the girl had someone she could talk to. Someone who would hear her the way Dax had heard Kenzi. School budgets had cut many of the counseling services, but the director said she'd follow up with her personally. She asked if Kenzi would speak at another school, and Kenzi agreed to discuss the possibility later in the week. Kenzi wasn't sure she wanted a public speaking career, but she now saw an area where she could make a difference. For as long as Kenzi could remember, her mother had been hosting fundraisers for a variety of organizations. Kenzi had always looked at them as an excuse for her mother to throw big parties, but it was more powerful than that. Her mother was already making a difference in the world. Kenzi vowed to soon feel the same way about herself.

Lexi and Willa hugged Kenzi as soon as she walked off the stage. "You were amazing," Willa said.

"You really were," Lexi added as she pulled her aside. "There's something you need to know, though. We didn't tell anyone you'd be here, but—"

"But?" Kenzi asked in a rush. She scanned the back of the auditorium for who she hoped would be there even though it made no sense that he would be. Her stomach did a nervous flip when she saw one of her brothers leaning against the back wall.

Kenzi squared her shoulders. *I'm going to hear it sooner or later anyway, so why not now?* "I should go talk to him. I won't be long, okay?"

"Take all the time you need," Willa said.

"Hey, there're three of us. If he gives you trouble we can take him," Lexi said with a wink.

"It's Lance," Kenzi said in resignation to her fate. "He won't yell at me, he'll just tell me all the reasons this wasn't a good idea and possibly suggest some ways we could squash the story before the media picks it up."

Willa looked from Lance to Kenzi. "We'll squash *him* if he is anything but supportive."

Kenzi chuckled at Willa's uncharacteristically aggressive comment. Most people were intimidated by her brothers, but Lexi and Willa never had been. That was one more reason Kenzi loved them. "I'll be right back."

The students had left by the time Kenzi made her way over to where her brother was standing. Kenzi prepared herself for whatever Lance would say. No matter how angry or how disappointed he was in her, she couldn't let it diminish how good she felt about what she'd just done. She stopped a couple feet from him. "Lance, before you say anything—"

Lance raised a hand and cut her off. His face was tight with anger. "How could I have not known? How could none of us have known?"

Kenzi shrugged helplessly. He'd heard her how and why. She didn't have answers beyond that.

"Dean knew, didn't he? That's why he—"

Kenzi nodded wordlessly.

Lance blinked twice, and his eyes looked glassy for a moment. "Kenzi, I don't know what to say."

Kenzi sniffed as her own eyes misted. "I had to do this, Lance."

With his hands clenched at his sides, Lance said, "I know. I mean, it all makes sense now. Dad asked us to give you some space to figure some stuff out. This is what you were figuring out, isn't it?"

Kenzi made a little face. "Yes."

"Dad thought it was about your birthday, because we didn't celebrate it."

Typical that my father thinks I'm worried about something that superficial—that narcissistic. Why wouldn't he? What have I ever done that mattered? When have I ever looked beyond myself?

"That did bother me, Lance, but it was all entwined with this. I feel badly that I didn't tell the family first, but I knew someone would try to stop me. I don't want to live a lie anymore. I don't want to be perfect anymore. I want to get angry sometimes and not worry that everything will fall apart if I raise my voice. I want to cry when I'm sad. Say what I want to say. Outside of our family people fight and forgive each other. They work things out. They don't hide everything they feel. I want to be like that, Lance. I tried the other way, and it was killing me. I know no one will be happy with what I did today, but I hope you respect that I had to do it."

Lance rubbed a hand roughly up his jaw. "Okay."

In surprise, Kenzi asked, "That's it? Okay? What does that even mean?"

Lance raised and lowered a shoulder. "It means I understand why you're doing this, and you have my support. If you need me to explain it to Mom and Dad, I will."

Kenzi clasped her hands in front of her as the love she had for her brother doubled. "No, I'll do it. The hardest part is behind me. I'm not afraid anymore."

He hugged her, and Kenzi took a moment to savor the calm before what would surely be a storm later with her family. She stepped back and said, "Lexi and Willa are taking me to lunch. Would you like to join us?"

Lance glanced over at her friends. "The way Willa is glaring at me I probably shouldn't. You go and enjoy yourself. I have to get back to the office."

A quick look confirmed that Lance had put the right name on the right twin. "She was just worried you'd say something to upset me."

Lance winked at Willa. "Tell her if she keeps frowning at me like that I'll stop considering her the prettier one."

With the tension falling away, Kenzi looked back at her two friends and said, "May I suggest you never have that conversation with either of them?"

Lance smiled, agreed, and left. Tempting as it was to tell Willa what Lance had said, Kenzi kept it to herself. If there was one thing she'd learned over the years, it was that comparisons between twins were never welcomed.

Kenzi spent a very enjoyable lunch with her friends at a sandwich shop near her house. She was tired when she said goodbye to them early in the afternoon, but she felt as if a huge weight had lifted from her. With that weight gone, she knew she could handle her family's reaction. She checked her mail on the way in and saw an envelope with just her name on it. She knew the handwriting.

Dax.

She tore the envelope open. The only thing written on the inside was an address. *His?*

Her hands were shaking as she dialed his number. "Dax?"

"How did it go?"

"Good. Really good." She paused. "Did you put a card in my mailbox?"

"Yes."

"There's nothing on it but an address."

"I know. I wrote it."

With her heart beating with excitement, Kenzi asked, "What's at that address?" *You?*

"You'll have to go to find out. I suggest you go soon, though."

"Should I take anything?" *Wear anything?*

"No, but call me later."

Call him? So he's not going to be there? Disappointment swept through her. "It's been a long day, Dax. I don't know. I appreciate whatever it is, but—"

"Do you trust me?"

"Yes," Kenzi said without hesitation.

"Then go."

DAX WAS SITTING at his desk still smiling a few minutes after he'd hung up with Kenzi. With Kate's help, he'd found a privately owned pet shop on Newbury Street and paid it to close for the day. Although the shop had claimed to have several breeds on hand, Dax wanted to make sure Kenzi was able to find exactly what she wanted, so he had several litters with impeccable pedigrees brought over from local breeders. Money was no option, and Dax was confident Kenzi would leave there with a new friend.

He couldn't wait to see if she chose one of the tiny dogs women often stuck in purses or a large breed that would protect her apartment. Whatever she chose, she'd have the dog he knew she'd wanted since childhood.

"Mr. Marshall?" Kate asked.

"Yes."

"Can I have a raise?"

Dax shook his head to clear it. "What was that?"

"You look so happy, I figured it might be a good time to ask."

"Happy, huh?"

His secretary smiled at him. "Very."

I feel happy. As the words popped into his head, he realized how true they were. In the past he'd done many things that had brought him satisfaction, but he couldn't remember feeling as good about anything as he felt about getting Kenzi a dog.

"So, I'll just write a proposal for my increase and have you sign off on it, okay?"

Dax stood and walked over to the window of his office and looked out over the city. He'd convinced himself that the best thing for Kenzi was to stay away from her, but what if that wasn't true? She said she felt better because he'd listened to her. He felt incredible every time he spoke to her . . . or even thought about her. Maybe he was wrong. Maybe she wouldn't hate him when it ended. "Sounds good," he said absently. "Cancel my meeting tonight. I'm leaving early."

Chapter Nine

KENZI EXITED THE cab onto the busy Newbury Street sidewalk. She double-checked the address on the card against the numbers on the buildings. Following a hunch, she went down a stairway and stood outside a pet store with a sign that read, "Closed for everyone but Kenzi."

The door swung open and a petite woman with wild red curls opened the door. "Kenzi?"

"That's me," Kenzi said with a smile. The woman said something else but Kenzi couldn't hear it over the barking behind her.

"Come in," the woman said quickly. "Please excuse the playpens and the noise. When your boyfriend asked if I'd let some breeders bring puppies here, I had no idea he meant so many. I've never seen anything like this."

Boyfriend? No. Kenzi didn't correct her. Labels weren't as important as how Dax made her feel. Maybe all they would ever be was friends, but what a beautiful friendship it was turning out to be.

The small boutique was wall-to-wall puppies. Big ones, tiny ones. Some were sleeping, some were wildly barking.

Kenzi felt like she'd walked into a dream. *Dax did this. For me.* She looked down at the nearest pen and saw the most adorable fluff of white hair. It looked too small to pick up so Kenzi bent down. It licked her hand and raced around like a tiny stuffed animal come to life.

"You can pick her up," the woman said. "She's a Maltese. The paperwork says her mother was five pounds and her father was four. She'll be tiny."

Kenzi cuddled her to her neck. She'd never held anything so delicate. She held her a few inches in front of her face and marveled at how brave the little pup was. She yipped and wagged her tail happily.

In the next pen she saw a puppy that was easily twenty times the size of the one she was holding. She put the white fluff down and picked up the yellow, short-haired Labrador puppy. It lapped at her face and squirmed in her arms with excitement.

The shopkeeper put on her glasses and read from a piece of paper. "That one isn't one of mine. He's twelve weeks old and from a line of show dogs. You can't find a more loyal dog than a Lab, but if you live in an apartment they need a lot of exercise. Regardless of which puppy you choose, payment has already been settled, so take your time and look around."

Kenzi was overwhelmed but happily so. *I'm getting a puppy.* She remembered the conversation she'd had about dogs with Dax. He'd said he didn't like them, but that hadn't stopped him for doing this for her. *On a day when I finally feel free to start living my life on my terms. What a perfect way to celebrate my new life.*

Another man might have picked out a puppy for her and chosen something he thought she'd want. Or worse, something his secretary thought she'd want. Dax wasn't like that. For all his talk about not caring about anyone but himself, he was one of the kindest and most considerate people she'd ever met.

She put the large puppy back in its pen. "I don't know where to even start. They're all so beautiful. I do live in an apartment though, so maybe a smaller breed would be better."

The woman reached down and picked up another tiny ball of fur. "Pomeranians are a popular choice. This one came in last week. He is probably the quietest puppy in here. Which is strange, but dogs also have personalities. If you're looking for one to cuddle with, I have a feeling this one will be a lapdog."

Kenzi took the puppy in her arms, and it settled against the crook of her neck with a sigh. Her heart swelled with love for it, and she was just about to tell the woman she'd made her choice when a movement near the counter caught her attention.

"Oh, excuse me," the shopkeeper said quickly. "I'll be just a minute." She went over to a small adult cocker spaniel that was standing beside a dog bed near the checkout counter. "Lay down, sweetie. I'm right here." The dog whined but laid back down on the bed.

Kenzi followed the woman over, still holding the tiny Pomeranian puppy to her. The cocker spaniel had been shaved down, but it was easy to see that it had bald spots. It had a bandage on one foot and a healing wound that circled its neck like a collar. When the woman realized Kenzi was watching, she said, "This is Taffy. I probably shouldn't have brought her today, but I hate to leave her alone. She's just learning to trust people again. She should be fine now."

"What happened to her?" Kenzi asked, unable to take her eyes off the dog, who looked completely out of place in the shop.

The woman looked down at the dog and shook her head sadly. "She's had it tough. She was found in Florida tied up on a tar surface with no shade. It burned the pads of her feet badly. She'd outgrown the collar around her neck so it was cutting into her and was infected. I'm a tech at a vet office, and one of the clients brought her in. She said she found her when she went down to visit her family and simply took her. Stole her, I guess. She wouldn't say. My guess is she knew the people. Anyway, she brought Taffy back with her, and that should have been Taffy's happily ever after, but the woman didn't realize how expensive a sick dog could be. Taffy's feet were infected, one more seriously than the others. Her skin is still sensitive from prolonged exposure to fleas and ticks. When the woman found out Taffy would need more care than she could afford, she asked us to put her down. I offered to take her. Taffy looks worse than she is, really. With some love and the right care, she might even be beautiful one day."

Kenzi handed the shopkeeper the puppy she'd been holding and sat on the floor beside Taffy. "She's beautiful now." Very carefully Kenzi offered her hand to the dog to sniff. Taffy licked her hand then stood.

"She'll sit on your lap if you stay there," the owner warned.

"She's welcome to." Kenzi rested her hands behind her, and Taffy stepped onto her lap and settled against her stomach. She was small but not as small as the designer puppies. Ten pounds or so. Thin. Kenzi gently ran her hands over Taffy, carefully avoiding the places that might have hurt the dog. "How old do you think she is?"

"She's young. I'd say two years maybe. She's spayed, which was another surprise. She's small for her breed, so she was probably starved, too. I'd like to think there is a special place in hell for whoever mistreated her."

Me, too.

There was a knock on the shop door and the woman excused herself to answer it. Kenzi stayed where she was, softly petting the dog who was now looking up at her with so much hopeful trust that Kenzi decided right then and there that Taffy was coming home with her.

A shadow fell over Kenzi, and she looked up to see Dax dressed in a dark business suit. Even amidst an ocean of barking puppies, he looked calmly in control and even more gorgeous than she remembered. He crouched down beside Kenzi and looked over the dog in her lap. Kenzi was about to try to justify her choice, when a smile spread across his face.

"You found your dog," he said and held his hand out. Taffy licked his hand then settled her head back onto Kenzi's leg.

It wasn't a question. There was no judgment or sarcasm. Kenzi looked to the shopkeeper. "If she's for sale, I did."

The woman smiled and wiped a tear. "She's free if you want her. She'll be shy at first. You'll have to work with her on that. When a dog has been through what she's been through, the trauma lingers."

I know exactly how that is. Kenzi looked back down at Taffy who was giving her that hopeful, sad look again. "What do you think, Taffy? Do you want to come home with me?"

Taffy raised her head and wagged her tail.

"You could take her now, but I have some of her medicine at my house. She'll be safe with me for one more night, and I can have everything organized and labeled for you when you come back tomorrow."

Kenzi's first impulse was to take Taffy right then, but the woman's plan made sense. It would also give Kenzi time to prepare her place for Taffy. "Tomorrow sounds fine."

"And if anything happens, all you have to do is call me."

Kenzi's eyes flew to the woman's. "I won't change my mind."

"Some people do."

"Not me," Kenzi said firmly. She directed her next words to the dog who was watching her intently. "Taffy, this is forever. My family is completely dysfunctional, but once you're one of us, there is no escape. You're stuck with us."

"That's one lucky dog." Dax offered Kenzi a hand up.

"I'm the one who is lucky . . . and grateful. This is the single nicest thing anyone has ever done for me. Thank you,

Dax." Kenzi eased Taffy off her lap and onto her bed then accepted Dax's help in getting back to her feet. Normally Kenzi would have brushed her backside off, but she was enjoying the feel of Dax's hand around hers too much to break the connection.

Dax told the woman he'd be in contact the next day. Kenzi arranged to pick Taffy up, chose all the necessary supplies, then they both exited the store. Kenzi was in front of Dax as they made their way up the steps.

Kenzi stopped abruptly, turned, and planted a kiss right on Dax's lips. It was meant to be a quick stolen kiss, one initiated in gratitude and affection, but as soon as their mouths met everything changed.

Dax cupped her face and deepened the kiss. Kenzi wrapped her arms around his neck and arched against him. It was everything a lover's first kiss should be and so much more than any Kenzi had ever experienced. It wasn't just her body that rejoiced at his nearness, her very soul yearned for him. She kissed him with the bottled-up passion of a woman who had resigned herself to wanting but never having him. He kissed her back with the hunger of a man who was giving in to a pleasure he'd denied himself.

When he broke the kiss off they were both breathing raggedly. "Kenzi, I don't ever want to hurt you, and I won't lie to you. I don't know what this is between us or how long it will last, but I want to be with you."

Dax was so serious, so genuine in both his desire and his concern for her that another piece of Kenzi's heart melted for him. "I want to be with you, too."

He kissed her lips hungrily then lifted his head again. "Are you sure? After this morning . . ."

Kenzi laid a hand gently on his cheek. "Telling my story didn't make me sad. It freed me. You freed me. I know you're worried that you'll hurt me, Dax, but I want this. I want you. For however long it lasts. Now, you can walk away again and leave us both gnawing off our limbs in frustration. Or you can come home with me and show me if you really are good enough to make me forget my name."

"Taxi," Dax joked with a huge smile.

Kenzi laughed when he spun her around and practically hauled her up the rest of the steps by the hand. The drive to her place was a test of restraint. They rode together in the back of Dax's town car holding hands and both barely breathing. Another man might have taken advantage of the time and his free hands, but Dax was waiting, and it made the drive even more intoxicating.

They rode up the elevator, barely breathing, doing nothing more than holding hands. As soon as the door of her apartment closed behind them, however, Dax hauled her to him, and the fire they'd held back for so long exploded, consuming them both.

With other men, she'd always held a part of her back, protecting herself. She didn't hold anything back with Dax. She trusted him in a way she'd never thought she could trust a man. It didn't matter if he couldn't promise her forever—he was hers that night.

Dax swung her up in his arms and carried her through the living room. He stopped kissing her just long enough to ask where her bedroom was. Kenzi impatiently waved a hand in the direction of her bedroom door. She didn't want to talk, she wanted his mouth on hers, his hands to continue their strong caresses. She needed it.

They kissed urgently all the way to her room. Kenzi pulled off his tie and had started on the buttons of his shirt when he placed her down on her feet and took her hands in his. "Easy, Kenzi. Take it slow."

Kenzi wanted to say they'd taken it as slowly as any human could endure, but one look at him changed her mind. There was a tender concern in his expression that brought an entirely new intimacy to what they were doing. He was a man who was used to taking, but with her he gave.

Because he cares about how I feel.

She took a deep breath and moved one of her hands to his still-clothed chest. His heart was beating wildly. Desire burned in his eyes, and Kenzi had never felt so close to a man. Dax wanted her to see she was in control of what happened to her, even here.

Kenzi held eye contact with him as she moved her hand lower and enjoyed the ridges of his stomach. He closed his eyes briefly in pleasure then opened to find her eyes again. She slid her hand even lower so her hand cupped his straining cock. He bent to kiss her neck while she caressed him. She whispered, "I want this, Dax. All of it. All of you. Don't hold back because you think I'm fragile. I'm not. Take me, Dax. Give me what you've been holding back."

One of his hands plunged into the hair on the back of her head, and he plundered her mouth with a kiss so intense

Kenzi thought she could orgasm before either of them had removed any clothing. She shifted to grip his shoulders and steady herself while one of his hands moved to her ass, grinding her forward against his excitement.

He lifted his head, and she saw how close he was to losing control. Kenzi unbuttoned her shirt quickly and dropped it to the floor. She unclasped her bra and dropped it as well.

He groaned and shifted her position so her legs were wrapped around his waist. He kissed the curve of her neck, down her newly bared shoulders, and between her breasts. Everywhere his lips went, his tongue teased. Kenzi was on fire. When he took one of her nipples between his teeth and gave it a gentle tug, she cried out, "Oh God, yes!"

He took his time with one breast then moved to the other until Kenzi was shaking with need. He stepped forward and eased her down onto the bed so she was lying flat, but her feet still rested on the floor. His mouth was hot and burning a trail of kisses across her stomach. He removed her shoes then continued to kiss her as his hands undid the fastening of her pants and pulled them off at the same time as her panties.

He dropped to his knees and positioned himself between Kenzi's legs. She gripped the bed sheets on either side of her in anticipation. He ran his hands up and down the length of her legs as he kissed the sensitive skin inside one of her thighs and then the other. She was near tears by the time she felt his hot breath on her sex, but still he took his time.

His hands gripped her thighs from above as he appreciated the view. "You're so goddamn perfect."

Kenzi shuddered. She was wet and ready for him. Instead of feeling exposed or vulnerable, she felt wonderfully, indescribably sexy. She rolled to a sitting position and pulled his face up to hers. Yes, she wanted what he was offering, but she wanted it on her terms, too. With him, she knew she could have both. Their tongues danced deeply together.

Dax slid a finger inside her wet slit. Kenzi gasped against his mouth when he found her clit and rolled it between his fingers. There was a strength to his touch that bordered on too much, but was actually, excruciatingly perfect.

She lay back on the bed, and he kissed his way downward. His fingers parted her lips and his mouth sought her already throbbing nub. Kenzi cried out again as he slid two fingers inside her and pumped in and out while his mouth worked its magic on her clit.

There was no past, no future, only pleasure and the need for release. Dax brought her to the edge of climax again and again only to pull away just before and kiss his way across her thighs again. Kenzi writhed on the bed, begging him to take her.

He stood, removed his clothing, and donned a condom. He rolled onto the bed with her, his huge cock grazing against the inside of her thighs as he settled himself above her. He kissed the space between her breasts. They kissed deeply again. With one hand he lifted her ass off the bed and entered her with a powerful thrust.

She tasted herself on his tongue and loved it in a way she'd never thought she would. She opened her legs and her mouth wider for him, giving herself over to him completely.

He filled her deeply, fully. It wasn't just the size of him, although he was beautifully endowed. He drove into her with controlled, strong thrusts that took her closer and closer to the climax she'd begged for earlier.

Her hands couldn't touch enough of him. She couldn't take him deeply enough into her. She jutted her hips up to meet his and the way he groaned into their kiss drove her even wilder beneath him.

When she finally came she was calling out his name again and again, his thrusts becoming as wild and uncontrolled as she felt. He made a feral sound and took one final plunge.

Kenzi collapsed, sweaty and spent. Dax held his weight off her even though they remained intimately connected. He looked down at her and smiled. "Kenzi."

Kenzi was floating on the warm aftermath of her orgasm. She smiled back dreamily. "Dax."

He rolled away briefly and cleaned himself. When he returned he took her into his arms and pulled a sheet over both of them. He was still smiling as he kissed her forehead. "Holy shit."

She cuddled her naked body against his. "I was thinking the same thing."

They lay comfortably against each other for a while, their breathing slowly returning to normal. Dax caressed Kenzi's back lightly. Kenzi rested her head on his shoulder, savoring the light scent of his cologne. The same one she'd given him that would forever meld with the memory of him inside her, of her calling out his name while she climaxed.

Now that's a good sales pitch for a cologne.

She smiled against his shoulder.

"What are you smiling about?" Dax asked.

She answered him honestly because he'd always done that with her. "I love your cologne. It's amazing."

He chuckled. "I didn't wear any today. That's me."

Kenzi sniffed his neck. "Well, then you smell amazing."

He rolled so he was half above her. "So do you, but you taste even better. I imagined this so many times." He cupped one of her breasts beneath the sheet. "But you're even more perfect than I imagined."

Kenzi touched his cheek gently. "I'm not perfect, Dax, I'm just me."

He growled in her ear. "How about sexy as hell and so addictive I can barely think of anything else."

Kenzi smiled and murmured against his lips, "I'll take that."

He kissed her neck. "What else do you like?" His cock nudged against one of her thighs as it came fully to attention again.

Boldly Kenzi wrapped a hand around his erection and pumped up and down. She'd never felt so free to be herself with a man. "I like you, Dax."

He raised his head and looked down at her intensely for a long moment. "I like you, too, Kenzi. This isn't a one-time thing for me."

They weren't exactly words of love, but Kenzi could tell they were more than Dax normally said. She continued to caress him with one hand while she pulled his mouth back to hers with her other.

Things with Dax were simple. No, he didn't promise her anything, but he also didn't demand anything. There was no guilt, no fear that either of them would hurt the other. For once she could simply let go and enjoy.

That's exactly what she did with Dax well into the night and then again the next morning. She gave herself over to the uninhibited bliss of sex with a man who cared about her with no strings and no expectations.

While showering with Dax, she marveled at how comfortable she was around him. She'd never felt so relaxed with a man.

They had a leisurely breakfast together and chatted about their plans for the day. Finally, Dax looked down at his watch, swore, and started gathering his wallet and phone.

Kenzi walked him to the door, and he gave her one final deep kiss. It wasn't until he said, "I'll call you," that Kenzi had a moment of panic.

He'd said that before—and hadn't.

She'd told herself she could accept him on his terms, but the idea of not hearing from him again sent a stabbing pain through her. She wanted to grab his arm and demand he keep that promise, then she remembered what he'd said about not believing in promises.

She kept her silence as much out of habit as respect for how he had accepted her, scars and all. He'd helped her find her voice, and now he'd shown her how good things could be with the right man. No matter what happened, she was glad he'd come into her life. "Bye, Dax," Kenzi said and closed the door. She slumped against it then took several deep breaths.

He'd said what they had wasn't a one-time thing.

He doesn't believe in getting attached. Will this end when he returns to London? Are we together until then? Is that what he meant?

DAX HAD LEFT Kenzi in the morning mostly because he'd never wanted to stay with anyone as much as he'd wanted to stay with her. He'd woken before her to the feeling of her bare body snuggled up against his and been spooked by how good it had felt. She wasn't the first woman who'd woken up beside him, but she was the first one he felt belonged there.

He'd awakened her with a kiss, and they'd made love slowly. It had been every bit as good as the wilder sex from the night before. He should have felt amazing, but his insides were churning. Kenzi had joined him in the shower and, although it had been a sexually charged experience, it had also been more. They'd talked and laughed in an easy way he wasn't used to. She wasn't just a woman he was having sex with.

But what did that make her?

There were times when he'd have said they were friends, although he didn't have female friends. He's always believed mixing friendship and sex made things too complicated, and he didn't like complicated.

Complicated was Kenzi's middle name.

He'd told her that what they had wasn't a one-time deal. He'd meant it. Being with her had only made him want to be with her again. He wanted to tell her he would be the only man in her life, the only one in her bed.

That sounded an awful lot like a relationship, and he didn't do those.

He'd told himself he could be with Kenzi without hurting her, but he wasn't so sure anymore. Whenever she looked at him he saw how little she knew him. He wasn't a kind man, not the way she thought he was. He could supply her with list after list of people who either feared or hated him, and it wasn't something that had bothered him before. People who thought success could be attained without personal cost were either inexperienced or stupid.

Dax changed at his office and tried to use work to clear his head. His thoughts kept going back to Kenzi. He wondered if she had Taffy yet. He knew she was planning to take her to a veterinarian before taking her home. He hoped she received good news about her health.

He thought about Dean Henderson and how he'd warned Dax to stay away from Kenzi. Once the news of what had happened to Kenzi got back to her family they'd see Dean in a different light. Everyone would. *I do.*

How would Kenzi's family react when they heard her secret? Would they rush to support her? She said they wanted to protect her. He knew her brothers by reputation. They were powerful men who were often just as ruthless as he was. How would they react to the news that they'd failed to protect one of their own?

With that in mind, Dax realized he hadn't seen Parker or Josh Draun the last time he'd been there. Usually a bodyguard was somewhere in the background, invisible to most, but there. Dax had his secretary hunt down Parker's number, and he called him. He was surprisingly tight-lipped about both why he'd been hired and when he'd been let go. It spoke volumes about his loyalty to Kenzi, but left Dax with an unsettled feeling.

Between meetings Dax located Grant Barrington's phone number. He'd spoken to Grant a few times in the past regarding investments. Grant had a solid reputation for speaking his mind and, from what Dax knew of the family, was the least hot-headed of the Barringtons.

Grant answered in a neutral business tone. "Dax Marshall. I've heard your name often lately. What can I do for you?"

"Grant. I'm calling on a personal matter."

"Go on."

"I need to know the reason your family hired a bodyguard for your sister. Was it based on a specific threat or general concern for her?"

Grant's first response was silence. He might have been waiting for Dax to explain why he felt he had the right to ask, but Dax didn't explain himself to anyone. Grant finally said, "I wasn't aware you knew my sister."

"That doesn't answer my question."

"I have no intention of answering anything until I hear how you know Kenzi."

"We're friends." That was the truth. As much truth as he'd reveal for Kenzi's sake. "Is she in any danger?"

"She has, as you've said, security watching her."

"Not anymore. Does she need it?"

"What do you mean not anymore?"

"She let him go. How about we stop playing twenty questions, and you tell me why he was hired in the first place?"

"Kenzi has never mentioned knowing you."

"I'd say there is a lot you don't know about your sister, but that's another matter. We both want the same thing, so give me the information I need, or I'll find it elsewhere."

"If there were a reason, what would you do?"

"I'd make sure she had protection she couldn't see or fire."

"Because you're friends?"

"Yes."

Grant was quiet for another long moment. "Our family received a few threats from abroad. They were linked to some recent family business in Trundaie. They may have been empty threats, but we weren't taking any chances when it came to Kenzi."

"Consider it covered. I have local people who are paid well to stay invisible."

Grant made a displeased sound, but wasn't going to argue the point. "What did you mean when you said there is a lot I don't know about Kenzi?"

"Are you close to her?"

"She's my sister."

"Are you close?"

"I don't know what you want me to say. In fact, there is not much about this conversation I understand or am comfortable with. Of course I'm close to my sister."

"She's going to need you soon. I don't know what you normally say or do, but don't do it this week."

"What are you talking about? Did something happen? If you hurt her—"

"I've said all I am going to say, but you seem to care about your sister. If you do, this is a good time to prove it." Dax hung up before Grant had a chance to ask him more.

He was irritated with himself for saying as much as he had to Kenzi's brother. Her story was hers to tell and how her family responded to the news, whenever they heard it, was none of his business. He hadn't planned to say anything to Grant about it when he'd called. All he'd needed to know was that Kenzi would be safe if he stepped away from her to clear his head. There was work piling up for him in London. He'd half decided already that a trip back would be the best for him and Kenzi.

When he'd spoken to Grant, though, he'd felt compelled to warn them Kenzi would need their support. From what she'd said, her family didn't handle things well. He wanted them to be there for her this time.

He thought back over the conversation he'd had with Grant and shook his head. *I don't get involved. What the fuck am I doing?*

His cell phone beeped with an incoming message. A photo of Taffy curled up on a footstool beside Kenzi's stocking feet came through with a message from her. **Taffy wants to say thank you for her new home. She is officially now the most spoiled dog in the Boston area. I hope it doesn't go to her head.**

Dax smiled and texted back. **What did the vet say?**

Nothing more than we already knew. Once he heard her story he thought she might try to bite someone when they looked her over, but she was a good girl. It was like she knew they were there to help her. I had a crash course in skin conditions and how to apply ointments and bandages. We're home now, though, and she looks happy to be here.

Kenzi's unasked question hung heavily in the air.

If she'd waited for him to call her that day, he wouldn't have. Or he might have. Hell, he didn't know. She had him so turned around he couldn't predict what he'd say or do next.

There was nothing sexy about a shot of Kenzi's foot beside the ugliest dog Dax had ever seen, but he couldn't stop looking at the photo. **What's your favorite takeout place?** She named a sushi place that was one of his favorites when he came to town. **I can be at your place at seven. Eat in?**

Yes. Her simple answer sent a wave of warmth through him and shot his plan to stay away from her for a few days straight to hell.

See you tonight, he texted back and threw his phone on his desk. Every time he thought he knew how to handle Kenzi, he was drawn back to her. He still thought the best thing he could do for her would be to end it early before she became too attached to him.

Seeing her again was a selfish decision on his part. He wanted back in her bed, back in her arms. The memory of her sweet taste brought his cock to full attention. He forced himself to stay and work. She was a heady distraction, but that kind of attraction didn't last.

He shouldn't give in to it.

He shouldn't let it control him.

But, God, he couldn't wait to see her again.

Chapter Ten

KENZI SNAPPED HER fingers, and Taffy moved up to sit on her lap on the couch. She petted her gently and said, "I know what you're thinking. He said he'd call me and I should have waited. That's the way the game is played. But I don't want to play games with him. I've never felt like this with anyone. I don't have to hide with him. I don't have to pretend. When I'm with him, I feel like I am finally me—the me I was supposed to be, and I can do anything. Is that crazy?" Taffy looked at her in adoration and wagged her tail. She scratched behind the dog's ear. "I shouldn't ask your opinion. I have a feeling you'd agree with anything I say today."

Kenzi reached over and took out a notebook. She made a list of what she wanted to do over the next few weeks. She definitely planned to speak to another school if the director thought her message was needed. She also intended to raise money for the school program. She looked down at Taffy and listed ways she could help animals that had been in her situation. The list included as many questions as it did action steps, but Kenzi felt empowered when she read it over.

Kenzi petted Taffy's head again. "You're going to heal up quickly, Taffy. When you do, don't be like me. Don't waste all your time thinking about yourself and wishing your life had been perfect. That won't make you happy. It doesn't change anything. But this"—Kenzi held up the notebook—"this is changing everything. We'll have to find a way for you to do some good when you are better. Would you like that?"

Taffy licked Kenzi's hand and cuddled closer. There were a hundred things Kenzi planned to do, but just then she was happy letting Taffy find comfort in her presence. She took out her tablet and read with her new friend happily tucked against her.

A while later, Kenzi's phone beeped with a message. It was from her father, and he said he was downstairs. Kenzi stood with Taffy in her arms and buzzed him in. She hadn't heard from her family since she'd made her speech at the school. Lance might have said something to her father, or her father might have heard about it in another way. There was a chance he didn't know anything and was coming to check in with her simply because she hadn't seen him recently.

As soon as her father stepped out of the elevator, Kenzi knew he knew. His expression was drawn tight, and he looked about ten years older. Angry or sad. Kenzi wasn't sure which. He looked both. "May I come in?" he asked.

"Of course," Kenzi said and held the door open beside her.

He sat down on her couch and slumped forward, his hands between his knees. He looked as if he was about to say something then stopped himself and ran a hand roughly over his face. Kenzi stood beside the chair across from him. She'd never seen her father look so upset. He's always been the rock of the family. She hated that she was the reason he looked broken.

He didn't meet her eyes. He looked at the floor in front of him and blinked several times. "When we lost your twin—Kent, I thought that was the worst pain I would ever feel. I couldn't make things better for Sophie. All I could do was try to hold the family together while she fell apart." He was quiet for few minutes as if memories from that time were more than he could bear. His face contorted with pain, and Kenzi almost stopped him and told him he didn't have to say it, but she didn't. The past needed to be faced, by Kenzi and by her father. "I never wanted any of us to go through that hell again. I tried to protect her from everything I thought could hurt her." He hit his thigh with a fist. "Maybe I went too far. You're right, it was all for Sophie."

Kenzi put Taffy down on the dog bed. "You did what you thought you had to do. I know that."

"When I think about what you went through and how we sent you away. How could you not hate us—me?"

"I don't hate you, Dad."

"I told your mother. She wanted to come, but I asked her to let me talk to you first. She was hurt when you said you needed time away from her, and then devastated when she heard what had happened to you. I'm worried about her. She doesn't understand how she missed it, and she feels like she let you down. It wasn't her, though. She doesn't know what I asked of all of you for her benefit. She would have never put her needs above yours. I did that, Kenzi. She loves you." He clasped his hands together and met her eyes. "I do, too."

Kenzi moved around the chair to sit down. "I know, Dad. How did you find out?"

"Lance took me aside and told me. I thought Asher had a sharp tongue, but Lance made sure I understood my role in your silence. It wasn't an easy pill to swallow, but I needed to hear everything he said. I understand now what you were trying to tell us. All I can say is I'm sorry, Kenzi. Sorry for all of it." His hand clenched on his knee. "I was so blind. I thought Dean was pulling you into a bad crowd. Lance said the boy he almost killed was the one who did this to you. Is that right?"

Kenzi nodded. "Dean warned me to stay away from him, but I didn't listen. He must have said something to Dean because I didn't."

"You should have told us," her father said huskily.

"I tried," Kenzi answered, her voice broke with emotion. There was more that Kenzi could have said, but she held it back. It didn't matter who had been right or wrong that day. Placing blame on either of them wouldn't change what had happened. It also wouldn't help them move past it. And that's what Kenzi wanted to do. She'd broken free of the hold the past had had on her. She didn't want to go back. "It's okay, Dad. *I'm* finally okay."

Dale nodded slowly. "Lance said your talk was amazing."

"That's what happens when you're the daughter of a politician. Public speaking must be in my blood."

"I want to say I'll go listen to you, but—"

Kenzi had never seen her father so close to tears. "You don't have to, Dad. I'm not even sure I'll do another talk like that. I needed to get the truth out there, but now that it is, I see that there are many ways I can help people. I thought I'd ask Mom to help me organize a fundraiser for the program I worked with."

Dale brought a shaky hand up to his forehead. "Your mother would love that."

To ease the tension of the moment, Kenzi snapped her fingers to call Taffy to her side. "Do you want to meet the newest addition to my family? This is Taffy. I got her today."

Dale leaned forward and gave Taffy another look. "I assumed you were watching her for someone."

"No, she's mine."

Dale looked the dog over. "She's—she's—"

"Healing, Dad. Just like me."

Dale cleared his throat before saying, "Where did you get her?"

"A friend of mine knew I wanted a dog. He surprised me with filling a pet shop with puppies for me to choose from. They were adorable, but when I saw Taffy I knew she was meant to be with me. Sometimes it's that simple."

"This friend of yours, do I know him?"

In the past Kenzi would have hedged or lied. Not anymore. "Dax Marshall."

Her father's eyes widened. He didn't look happy with the news. "I know him by reputation only."

Kenzi shrugged. "I don't know his reputation, but he has

been a good friend to me."

Her father didn't say anymore on the subject. He stood and walked over to a photo Kenzi had of her with her brothers when they were younger. "What do you need, Kenzi? What can I do now that would make any of this right?"

"Time to figure myself out. That's all. And I need to know that you still love me. I tried to be the perfect daughter, Dad. I really did."

Dale turned from the photo, and this time there were tears in his yes. "Oh, baby, nothing could ever change how much I love you. You didn't do anything wrong."

Kenzi let out a long breath. "I didn't know if you'd all be angry that the story went public. I know Ian is always trying to keep our personal lives out of the papers."

"No one is anything but concerned about you, Kenzi."

She wished she could believe that. Kenzi looked up at the ceiling in frustration. "I'm not Mom. I can handle the truth."

"That is the truth. Everyone in the family knows now except Andrew. We didn't want him distracted, but I have a feeling he'll react the same as we all did. We thought we'd kept you safe, Kenzi. A part of me died when I realized how I'd failed you."

Kenzi crossed to stand beside her father. "It wasn't your fault, Dad. Just like it wasn't mine. Bad things happen, and who can make sense of why? But good things happen, too. I'm finally in a place where I can see that."

The buzzer surprised both of them. Kenzi rushed to the

door. *Oh, no, don't let it be.*

"It's Dax. Buzz me in."

Kenzi looked across to her father who held her gaze steadily. He wasn't going anywhere. Taffy padded over to stand beside Kenzi. She met the dog's eyes. "Well, do you have any idea how to get out of this? No, me either."

A SLIM WOMAN kept giving Dax looks as they rode up in the elevator together. He ignored her. He had a bouquet of assorted flowers in one hand, a gift bag in the other hand, takeout being delivered soon, and a big happy grin on his face. In a few minutes he'd step into Kenzi's apartment and pull her into his arms. Nothing else mattered. The other woman exited the elevator a floor before Kenzi's with one final lingering stare. Dax shrugged dismissively.

Taken.

The word was still echoing in his head when he stepped out onto Kenzi's floor. The woman in the elevator had been beautiful, but he hadn't felt anything when he'd noted that. Women had always come to him. Money did that. He was used to picking and choosing as he pleased. What he wasn't used to was the growing realization that there was only one woman he wanted. Kenzi.

Kenzi opened the door to her apartment and, still holding the gift bag in one hand and the bouquet in his other, he pulled her to him and kissed her with all the passion that had been building within him during their short separation. Although it had only been hours since he'd seen her, their reunion felt as if it had been much longer. He couldn't get enough of her. He stepped forward and kicked the door closed behind him.

The presents could wait. Well, most of them could. He had stopped and bought an intimate one he thought she might enjoy. He didn't know if she used toys, but in his experience most women did and the idea of watching her orgasm again and again while he watched had him sporting a painful hard-on.

He dropped the flowers and the gift bag. She felt so damn good against him. To his surprise, after kissing him deeply at first, she pulled back—somewhat frantically. He instantly worried that he'd come on too strong. "I'm sorry, Kenzi. I lose my head around you."

She was breathing as heavily as he was, but she had her hands on his chest pushing him back. "My father's here, Dax."

"Your what?" He raised his head and looked behind her. There was indeed a very pinched-faced man watching them from the other room. *If looks could kill—*

She turned and picked up the items he'd dropped. "My father. He dropped by." She smiled and smelled the flowers. "They're beautiful." She held out the bag. "Is this for me, too?" She saw the dog bone inside and pulled it out. "Taffy, your first present." Taffy came over and took the bone delicately, as if she couldn't believe it was for her. "Is this for her, too?" Kenzi reached for the small, wrapped box still in the bag.

"No." Dax grabbed the bag from her and placed it on the floor beside the door. "You can open that later. Your father looks impatient to know who just mauled his daughter right in front of him."

Kenzi took his hand in hers. "I told him about you."

Dax looked down at her quickly.

"I said we're friends."

Dax met the other man's eyes. *Friends.* Kenzi's father looked far from believing that story. A thought occurred to him and he asked, "Is he here because he found out about yesterday?"

"Yes."

"And?"

Kenzi smiled up at him in the way that always sent his thoughts scattering. "And it's good. Better than I thought it would be. We talked. I'll tell you later."

"I'm glad." Dax was. He wasn't sure how Kenzi's happiness had become linked to his own, but it had. He didn't care what her father thought of him or would say to him as long as his visit had been what Kenzi needed.

Dale Barrington wasn't a powerful man on his own, but he was connected to the most influential families on the East Coast and his sons had become influential players in several financial fields. Most men would tread carefully for those reasons alone.

Dax wasn't most men. A potential clash with the Barringtons on a personal or professional level didn't intimidate him. Since meeting Kenzi, Dax had looked into her family extensively. He knew about the scandal that had cost Dale his political career. A man like Dale was no better than his father—weak and lacking in integrity. Dale had stayed with his wife, but he hadn't been faithful. Dax didn't personally have much respect for him, but he was Kenzi's father.

With Kenzi at his side, Dax walked over and held his hand out to Dale. "It's a pleasure to meet you, sir."

There was no warmth in Dale's eyes but he shook Dax's hand. "Marshall."

Kenzi stood beside Dax, watching them both. "His name is Dax, Dad."

Dale kept his attention on Dax. "I'd like to speak to Dax alone for a minute."

Dax nodded once. *Bring it on.*

Kenzi's hand closed around Dax's. "Whatever you have to say, Dad, say in front of me."

Dale pressed his lips together in a line of clear displeasure, then he said, "I'd rather not."

Dax felt the tension coursing through Kenzi. If she were confronting anyone but her father, he would have threatened the man, but Kenzi didn't need his protection just then. Dax didn't consider himself good at family issues, but if there was one thing he'd learned by being, however temporarily, part of so many it was that people needed to define their own relationships with each other. If handled by someone else, the conflict returned as soon as the enforcer of the peace stepped away. Dax gave Kenzi's hand a squeeze and kept silent.

Kenzi squared her shoulders. "Dad, do you trust me?"

Dale held eye contact with Dax. "*You,* yes."

"Then trust that I'm intelligent enough to know who is good for me and who isn't."

Dale directed his question to Dax. "What would you say if you found out a daughter of yours was dating someone like you?"

"Dad," Kenzi said in protest.

Several cutting comebacks flew to the tip of Dax's tongue. He could easily fire back that a father might think the same about a man with Dale's track record, but Dax kept his temper in check. Kenzi was puffing up protectively, defending him to her father, in a way that only one person in his life ever had. He'd take a bullet for Clay, and in that moment he realized he'd do the same for Kenzi. Even if the bullets that day were not so subtle insults from Dale. "I don't have a daughter so it's hard to say."

"Then let me help you. I know why you came to Boston, and I don't like it. I don't want you around my daughter or my family."

Kenzi said, "Dad, stop."

Dale looked at his daughter. "Did he tell you why he's here? He's after the Henderson's company. The biggest favor you could do Dean is to stay away from the man who is probably using you to get information about him."

"That's not true." Kenzi spun to look at Dax. "Tell him it's not true, Dax. You're not after Poly-Shyn."

With anyone else Dax would have walked away. As a rule, he didn't explain himself. "I told you there was a project here that was complicated. The company was initially for sale, but it was stable and the price was inflated. I wasn't interested. Recently confidence in the company has been shaken by indecisiveness at the top. Its value is spiraling downward. I looked into acquiring it. Right now it's a deal that's difficult to pass on, but I'm not moving forward with it."

"Because?" Kenzi asked.

"You know why," Dax answered gently.

Kenzi nodded slowly. "Because of Dean."

"Because of you," Dax corrected. It was an easy admission to make. He didn't believe in forever, but he did believe in honesty. He met Dale's eyes and said, "And because very few men impress me. I won't be the reason Dean Henderson loses his father's company."

Dale didn't conceal his disbelief. "You expect me to believe—?"

"I don't expect anything from you," Dax said, cutting him off as his temper rose. "Sir." He added the tag, but it also came out too aggressively to be respectful.

Kenzi gave Dax's arm a tug. He looked down at her, and the anger that had swept through him dissolved as quickly as it had come. She believed him. His heart swelled in his chest when she said, "Thank you."

Despite how her father was looking on, Dax pulled her against his side and kissed her forehead. He didn't have the words to articulate how she made him feel, so he didn't try. He just held her there for a moment and breathed in the sweet scent of her.

When he finally looked back at Dale there was a guarded expression on the man's face. The cold rejection of earlier was gone.

Kenzi turned back toward her father. "Dad, emotions are

running high right now. I don't want to fight with you, but I also don't want to pretend or lie anymore. Dax and I are friends. I need you to respect that. If we're more than that, it's our business. All you really need to know is that I care about this man, and I trust him. He's been good to me."

The buzzer on the wall went off. Dax nodded toward the door. "I ordered sushi."

Kenzi didn't look like she wanted to leave his side, but she did. "I'll buzz him in."

As soon as she stepped away, Dale said, "If you hurt Kenzi, I'll kill you."

Dax arched one eyebrow. "Let's hope it doesn't come to that."

"Do you think I'm joking?"

"No, sir, I don't."

"What are you doing with my daughter?"

Dax didn't answer that one. He didn't see how the truth would help.

Dale continued, "Are you in love with her?"

"With all due respect, Dale, love isn't a word in my vocabulary." Dale's eyes narrowed, but Dax continued, "The rest, as Kenzi said, is our business."

Kenzi cleared her throat behind them. She was close enough to have heard Dax's answer to her father's question. The tight smile on her face said she had. Part of him wanted to deny what he'd said, tell her . . . anything that would bring the smile back to her eyes. Instead he gave her a long unapologetic look and took the bag of food from her.

Kenzi stood there blinking as she sorted out her reaction.

Finally she looked at her father and asked, "Would you like to stay for dinner?"

Dale had a carefully neutral expression on his face. "No, your mother is expecting me."

"Tell her I'll come by the house tomorrow morning."

Dale didn't look happy about leaving, but he didn't have much choice. He hugged Kenzi then gave Dax one last meaningful glare. It would have been funny if Kenzi hadn't looked as conflicted as she did. She wanted her father to be happy and to respect her decision. From what Dax had seen it was one or the other with her family. He didn't like that. "I'll go with you tomorrow, Kenzi."

Kenzi's eyes rounded with surprise. "You want to meet my mother?"

"If *you* want me to."

A cautious smile split Kenzi's face. "She'll be curious about you, so that would actually be really nice."

Dale inhaled audibly but didn't say whatever he was thinking. He gave Kenzi a kiss on the cheek. "See you both tomorrow, then."

The look he gave Dax just before he left was as if he was trying to figure him out. Dax could have told him it was a waste of time.

None of this makes sense to me, either.

Sir.

Chapter Eleven

A S SOON AS her father was gone, Kenzi turned to Dax. "Sorry about that."

Dax placed the bag of food on the coffee table in the living room. He walked to where Kenzi was standing and took her in his arms. "Don't worry about me."

She melted against him, loving his strength. "I will if I want to."

He chuckled and kissed her temple. "I'm getting that sense about you."

Kenzi arched her neck back so she could look at Dax. She remembered what he'd said to her father about love not being in his vocabulary. He'd meant it. Dax equated love with his father's string of marriages. He hadn't said he loved her, and maybe that was a good thing. Whatever this was, it was more real than anything she'd experienced before.

Love is just a four-letter word people say too easily and rarely mean.

Dax and I are friends.
We care about each other . . .
That's what matters.

Dax lowered his mouth to the exposed curve of her neck and kissed his way up to her ear. Desire shot through Kenzi as her body readied itself for him. *Oh, yes, and there's that.*

His breath was a hot tickle on her ear as he asked, "Are you curious about your other gift?"

Kenzi was already unbuttoning the front of his shirt. "I will be later."

Dax removed his suit jacket and shirt, and Kenzi bit her bottom lip at the beauty of him. He stepped out of his shoes and socks and stood there smiling at her as if he could read her thoughts. Her naughty, "God, I hope he screws me all night" thoughts. Kenzi ran her hands up his strong arms and down his muscled chest. *I don't care how we label this, it's too good to ruin by overthinking it.*

Dax made record time removing her clothing before stepping out of the rest of his. Right there in her living room, they kissed and explored each other's bodies with a slow wonderment, as if it were their first time. The taste of him filled her senses. The strength of him made her eager to feel him above her, thrusting down into her. Like him, she took her time, because it was too good to rush. Every kiss, every caress, was so intense it moved Kenzi almost to tears. She'd never been with a man who felt so *right*.

Wanting him to feel as good as she was feeling, Kenzi sank to her knees in front of him and took his manhood in her hands with the intention of taking him into her mouth. He gripped the sides of her head, stopping her almost before she started. "Do you know what I want even more than to come in your mouth?"

Kenzi froze and shook her head. She was sexually experienced, but there were things on her list she'd never done, wasn't sure she'd ever do. She didn't know if he was about to ask her to do one of those things.

He dipped his thumb into her mouth then ran it across her open lips. "I want you so out of your mind that you can't take me deep enough, that you'll come while I do. Or so damn close it doesn't matter. Then I want to watch you come again because you help yourself."

Kenzi flicked his thumb with the tip of her tongue. "Yes."

"Then get my present."

Present? What present? Then she remembered the bag near the door. He helped her to her feet, and she went to retrieve it. Inside the bag she found a small rectangular box. She walked back to him and opened it. It wasn't the first silver bullet she'd ever seen, but it was the first one a man had ever given her. She'd talked to a boyfriend about toys once, and he'd gotten defensive, as if they would be competition. She'd never mentioned them after that. Dax was different. He was confident and wanted to ensure her pleasure while she pleasured him. The one he'd chosen was simple and non-threatening. She held it up and asked cheekily, "No bunny?"

He pulled her against him again, cupping her ass with his hands while his hard cock jutted against her stomach as he growled into her ear, "Do you want to try it? I want you to right now."

All joking fell to the wayside. She loved when he spoke

to her that way. He knew what he wanted, and because she trusted him completely she found his demands sexy. "Let's do it."

Dax took it from her and walked them both over to one of her couches. He sat down, pulled her in front of him, and lifted one of her legs so her foot rested on the couch beside him. She steadied herself with a hand on his shoulder and gloried in being spread wide for him. He turned the bullet vibrator on and ran it first along the inside of her thighs, then across the mound of her sex. Kenzi bent to kiss him hungrily. His tongue fucked her mouth thoroughly while he eased the tip of it between her wet lips.

He settled the toy on her clit and slid two fingers inside her. He moved them deeper and deeper. Kenzi sighed with pleasure into his kiss. He eased his fingers out and back in slowly, then with more speed. Kenzi thought she'd come right then, but before she could he broke off their kiss. He moved one of her hands over the vibrator and said, "Show me what you like, but don't come. Save that for me, Kenzi."

As he watched, Kenzi moved the bullet back and forth over herself, adjusting it so it rested perfectly against the spot she knew would send her over the top. As she approached orgasm again, Dax said, "Get on your knees, but don't stop. You come when I come, Kenzi. Only when I come. Do that for me."

Near to speechlessly aroused, Kenzi would have promised him anything. She was far beyond thinking. She sank to her knees. He adjusted her position so he could resume using the bullet while she gave him what she hoped was an equally amazing blow job. She'd performed oral sex before and would have said that she didn't dislike it. It was something men loved. This time was different. Her body was wildly excited, and she wasn't thinking about technique, daydreaming, waiting for it to be over. She was on fire for Dax and sucked him with all the feral need burning through her. She raised and lowered her mouth onto him while he thrust a finger inside her. She couldn't get enough of him as she again approached climax.

He gripped the hair on the back of her head and said, "Now, Kenzi. I'm going to come. Come with me."

She heard him and joined him as if it were the most natural thing to obey a command to orgasm. She swallowed his juices while hers flowed down his hand, and even with him in her mouth, she made wild noises as she climaxed.

She raised her head and met his eyes. "Oh, my God, that was amazing."

"We're not done," he ordered softly. He held a hand out to her. "Come up here."

She held her toy against herself then straddled his spread knees. His hand went between her legs and took over again. "Come for me again, Kenzi."

Kenzi balanced herself by holding onto his shoulders while he slid the bullet lengthwise between her lower lips. He slid it inside her, then out, and back and forth lengthwise again.

Kenzi arched in excitement, and he took one of her breasts into his mouth, sucking then circling her nipple with his tongue. He played her body with expertise until she was once again shaking with need.

Just as she approached another climax, he removed the bullet and eased her back onto her feet. He stood, put on a condom, then turned her toward the couch and eased her forward until she was bent before him.

Kenzi closed her eyes and cried out at how good he felt when he drove himself into her from behind. No toy could compare to how well he filled her, how powerfully he claimed her. He cupped her breasts and swore softly into her ear as he lost control finally and pounded into her sex.

He pulled out, turned her, and pushed her back so her back rested on the arm and back of the couch while her feet were on the floor. He lifted her feet, spread her legs wide and thrust into her deeply.

Kenzi came, screaming his name. He continued to pound into her a few more times before he came with a final thrust.

Dax pulled out, cleaned off, then lifted her into his arms and carried her to bed. He laid her gently down, covered her with the bed sheet, and joined her beneath them. Kenzi snuggled against him, and he kissed her cheek and groaned.

She hugged him tightly. "You have good taste in presents."

"And you have a fucking amazing mouth."

They lay tangled for a long time, coming back to earth together and simply enjoying holding each other. Although it wasn't yet night, they dozed.

Kenzi woke to her phone ringing. She ignored it at first but it rang again. She slid out from beneath a still-sleeping

Dax and went to find it.

When she looked at who was calling and checked her text messages, she wished she hadn't. Her father must have said something to her brothers because they were not only trying to get in touch with her, but they were saying they'd be there the next morning when she brought Dax by.

She looked up and saw the silver bullet he'd bought her still lying next to the couch. She cleaned it off, put it away, and gathered up the clothes she and Dax had shed all over her living room. No one was saying they'd drop by, but with her family anything was possible.

Breakfast with her brothers? Dax hadn't signed up for that. Would he back out?

There wasn't an ice cube's chance in hell that a meeting between her brothers and Dax would go well. They'd hated everyone she'd ever dated.

I can't do that to Dax.

DAX WOKE TO Kenzi climbing back into bed beside him. He tucked her back against his side and stroked her hair in wonder. When he wasn't with her he could almost convince himself he could walk away from her. But when she was with him she felt as vital to him as air.

It was scary shit.

And amazing.

She wasn't fragile anymore. Had she ever been? The past might have knocked her down, but in the short time he'd known her, she'd found her footing. He wouldn't say she was changing, but she was standing straighter, smiling easier.

She was also fucking incredible in bed; he didn't know how he'd go back to being with other women. He couldn't imagine ever wanting to. The idea was less scary every time he thought about it.

It was more than the sex, though. It was the way she'd stood up to her father, winning the argument without feeling that she had to hurt anyone to do it. It was the way she'd chosen Taffy instead of a purebred puppy almost everyone else he knew would have preferred.

Kenzi Barrington was a good person, a better one than he was. Better than almost everyone he knew.

He remembered her face when she'd heard him say love wasn't in his vocabulary. For the first time in his life he wished it were. Life didn't work that way, though. He'd done many things a man with a conscience would regret. No, he'd never lied to anyone, but he'd also never shown mercy. In business, as well as in his personal life, he'd never taken into account how others felt. He'd always believed that, at the end of the day, even a friend like Clay would betray him.

Clay never had, and being with Kenzi made Dax wish he'd appreciated that earlier. He'd considered Clay the closest thing to family he had, but even that hadn't afforded him the loyalty it should have. Why should he when one day he'd disappoint him as well?

And Dean Henderson.

Another man might have been jealous of him, but Kenzi's eyes didn't light up when she mentioned him. He believed she genuinely felt guilty that Dean had kept his silence to protect her, and she'd never done anything to clear his name.

Kenzi caressed Dax's chest. "You don't look happy."

"I'm thinking."

"About what?"

"About your friend Dean."

"Oh." Her expression turned cautious. "He and I were never anything but friends."

Friends.

Dax suddenly didn't like how he also shared that title.

Kenzi touched his temple. "Now you're frowning. You believe me, don't you? I wouldn't lie about something like that."

"I believe you." *I just don't like it.* "Do you ever see him?"

Kenzi shook her head. "My parents really didn't want me around him, so I stayed away. I feel like I should say something to him now, so he'd know how grateful I am, but I haven't spoken to him since I moved away."

Dax's hand tightened on Kenzi's lower back. "I'll talk to him."

Kenzi's eyes flew to Dax's. "You? What would you say?"

Dax hadn't thought that far ahead. His comment had been a knee-jerk reaction to not wanting her to go to Dean, looking for a way to make an old wrong up to him. "He's going to lose his company if he doesn't do something soon. The writing is on the wall."

Kenzi went up onto one elbow and looked down at him in shocked surprise. "You'd help him?"

Fuck. Is that what I'm saying?

"I could offer him some advice." Dax closed his eyes briefly as he imagined how well that would be received by Dean.

Kenzi's eyes filled with tears. "You don't know how much that would mean to me. If I knew I was somehow able to repay Dean—" Her voice broke, and she shook her head. "Dax, you are the most wonderful man I've ever met." She kissed him then, effectively wiping Dean and everything else out of Dax's thoughts. Her breasts bounced against his chest as he pulled her on top of him.

It didn't take more than that for talking to be replaced by frenzied kissing. They rolled so she was beneath him, and Dax let everything else fall away. Tonight was about being with Kenzi, and he wasn't about to waste a moment of it thinking about another man.

In fact, he wasn't going to think about anything besides how to get Kenzi begging for him to take her again. And again. And then tomorrow morning, once again if they could still move.

Chapter Twelve

KENZI HADN'T FOUND the right moment the night before to tell Dax that her brothers would be at her parents' house, waiting for them. She tried to tell him several times while they got dressed that morning. Dax had his driver bring him fresh clothes, and there was plenty of time to say something while they waited. Kenzi simply didn't know what to say.

She didn't want to make it seem like he shouldn't go, but then she didn't want him to feel he had to. Ever since she'd come home as an adult, her brothers had driven away every man she'd introduced them to. She knew not to take anyone home to meet her parents, but that didn't stop her brothers from showing up at a restaurant she was eating at or a social gathering. Lance would appear first and ask a hundred questions about her date's personal life. Ian would attempt to smooth the situation over, but he could be just as bad when it came to making what would have been a conversation into an interrogation. If that didn't scare the guy off, Asher would take him aside and threaten him with something. Kenzi didn't know what since no one ever said, but the guy always came back looking shaken. If he stayed around by some miracle, Grant would lecture him on the importance of financial planning and stability. That was usually the last straw. Andrew wasn't around much, but if he was he had no problem threatening her date's life right in front of her. As a rule, men were best hidden from her family.

Kenzi couldn't imagine Dax answering many of Lance's questions. Nor could she see him being intimidated by Asher. He seemed like the type who would debate financial strategies with Grant. She didn't know what Dax thought about the Marines, but she had the feeling he'd respect them.

So what am I afraid of? If Dax doesn't want to meet them, he'll say so. If he does, they won't get the best of him. They couldn't drive him away—could they?

There it is. The reason I haven't told him.

I want him to want to meet them, but what if, like all the other men who've met my family, he walks? I couldn't blame him.

What if Dax isn't as strong as I think he is? What if he's just a wonderful man who, after he meets my family, decides I'm not worth the hassle?

"Are you ready?" Dax asked as he straightened his tie. Perfectly groomed and dressed in his dark suit, he looked like he could hold his own with anyone's family. She wanted to believe the strength she sensed in him, but he'd told her on several occasions he didn't like complicated and that's what her family was. "Dax, I need to tell you something. I should have told you earlier."

He paused while putting his watch on. "I'm listening."

Here goes. "My brothers heard you'll be at my parents' house, so they're going to be there as well."

He finished securing his watch.

"All of them," she stressed.

He picked his phone off the table and put it into the breast pocket of his suit then held her gaze with a carefully blank expression that was often his first response. The man she wanted to talk to was the one he hid behind that wall. Kenzi waved a hand in the air for emphasis. "Imagine my father, but a hundred times worse. I don't know what they'll say to you, but some of it might not be very nice. You don't have to put yourself through this if you don't want to. It's one thing to meet my mother, but you don't know how bad my brothers can be." When he still didn't look impressed, she added, "Meeting them tends to end any relationship I'm in. I don't want to lose you because they—"

Dax closed the distance between them and cupped her chin with one of his hands. "So tell them to shut the fuck up."

The blunt way he said it had Kenzi choking on a shocked laugh. "I couldn't."

A smile curled Dax's lips. "You'd say it nicer than I would, but I saw you with your father. You're stronger than you think you are. You told him exactly what you needed from him. It sounds like your brothers need the same talk."

"They'd never—" Kenzi stopped herself there. Dax was right. She had been focused on his reaction to her brothers' behavior, but taking charge of her life wasn't just about talking about the past. She needed to stand up to her brothers, not just for Dax, but for herself. "You're right. I won't let them drive you away."

Dax ran a hand through her hair. "Let's be clear about something: there is nothing they could say to me that would end our—" He stopped as if the correct word eluded him. "I won't go if you don't want me to, but if you do, remember that they don't matter to me. What they say doesn't matter. I'll tell them all where to shove it if that's what you need me to do, but I have a feeling that's not what you'd want to see today."

"I do want you to go, and no, I wouldn't want that." Kenzi wanted to throw her arms around Dax. He was walking into an emotional battlefield, and his concern was how it would affect her. The words "I love you" would have been easy to say in that moment, but Kenzi held them back. He wasn't ready to hear them, and what they had was too new. Once said, those three words were impossible to take back. Kenzi looked down at Taffy who was giving her the saddest look from her dog bed. "Would you mind if I took Taffy in your town car?"

His answer was a snap of his fingers similar to how she'd called Taffy to her side so often. Taffy rushed to his side, favoring her still bandaged foot, but she was wagging her tail. He frowned down at her. "Do not make a mess in my car, do you understand?"

Taffy whined and wagged her tail harder. She could see past his tough exterior as easily as Kenzi could.

"I'll bring a towel," Kenzi said quickly. "Or we could call a different car service."

He continued to look down at little dog. "No, Taffy and I have an understanding."

"If you're sure," Kenzi said with a smile. She left the two of them briefly to put some treats, Taffy's leash, and a towel in a bag just to be safe. When she returned Taffy was still looking up at Dax with open adoration. It was remarkable that Taffy trusted anyone, considering what she'd been through, but Dax had strength that was easy to trust. *I like him, too, Taffy.*

A few minutes later, Kenzi and Dax were settled into the backseat of his town car. Taffy was on a towel on Kenzi's lap. Although she was headed off into what looked like it would be an emotionally charged family gathering, Kenzi wasn't scared. Dax was checking his email on his phone, but he was at her side. Taffy still looked like she'd survived a war, but she trusted Kenzi and Dax enough to be excited about going somewhere with them. Kenzi laid her hand on the dog's back and found strength in her visible injuries. *You're so brave, Taffy. I haven't always been, but I'm working on it.*

Kenzi looked at Dax and said, "You'll like my mother. I've never heard her say an unkind word to anyone."

Dax pocketed his phone and took her hand in one of his. "She passed that trait down to you."

Kenzi shrugged. "Yes and no. I think nice comes naturally to her. I didn't have much of a choice."

Dax arched an eyebrow. "Is she mentally unstable?"

It was a harsh question to ask, but Kenzi had gotten used to Dax speaking his mind with her. His honesty was one of the many things she loved about him. "I don't think so. She might have been right after my twin died, but that was a long time ago. Every year she falls into a kind of a depression during the month we were born, but I don't know what I'd be like if I ever lost a child. Every year my brothers and I would spend a week at my parents' house and wait it out. This past year, my brother Asher brought Emily home. My mother adores her, so it was a better year than most."

"Do you like her?"

"My mother?"

"Emily."

"I did when I first met her. Truth? My parents listen to her in a way they've never listened to me. If she says she thinks something is a good idea, we end up doing it. Asher has always been a bit overbearing, and I can almost handle that, but it's hard to stomach being forced to jump every time his fiancée thinks we should."

"Who is forcing you?"

"In our family we tend to do whatever makes my mother happy."

"Or?"

Kenzi shrugged. "Or we'd shoulder the guilt of having disappointed our father and hurt our mother."

Dax nodded. "My uncle who took me in after my father died was a very controlling man. It was his fist, not guilt, that he used to keep me in line. I wasn't sad when he died."

Kenzi laced her fingers with his and kept her silence. This was the Dax she knew he kept hidden from the world.

"I didn't miss my father after he died, either. He was never there for me. The only time he spent with me was when he wanted a woman to believe he was a good father, and afterward he'd drop me back off at school. I wouldn't hear from him until he wanted to put on a show again." He looked out the window as he spoke. "I don't know your parents, but your father seemed to care about you. I imagine he'd want a daughter who would miss him. Your mother sounds the same way. If you let them control you, you'll rob them of that."

Kenzi's took a long, shaky breath. Whenever she thought she couldn't be more grateful to Dax, he said or did something that revealed how much he cared. He wasn't sharing his pain to make himself feel better, he was opening himself to her because he wanted her to have something he'd never had. Tears filled Kenzi's eyes. *Love may not be in your vocabulary, Dax, but it's in your heart.*

When they pulled up to her parents' home, Kenzi handed Taffy and the towel to Dax. "Do you mind if I go in first? I need a few minutes alone with my family."

Dax was probably the only man who could still look drop-dead sexy and perfectly in command while holding a half bald dog. "Take your time."

Feeling spontaneous and more than a little grateful, Kenzi gave Dax a long deep kiss before moving toward the door his driver held open.

Dax smiled. "Or hurry. I told the office I wasn't coming in today."

And I'm dragging him to meet my family? Am I crazy? Kenzi flushed as her body hummed with anticipation of being in his arms again. She shook her head and reminded herself that all of this was part of her journey. If she ran and hid with him she would never become the woman she wanted to be.

"We don't have to stay long."

Dax didn't say anything, but she knew he'd stay as long as she needed him to. Having him in her life not only gave her confidence, but it also changed her perspective about some things. She did resent the way her family overrode her plans. She resented how effectively they'd silenced her, how not wanting to disappoint them had guided so many of her decisions. No, she didn't want to hurt them, but she didn't want to hate them, either. She wasn't a child anymore. *But I'm letting them treat me like one. Dax is right, I'm resenting them for something that I do have control over.*

She squared her shoulders as she opened the door of her parents' home. Her father met her and gave her a kiss on the cheek.

Dale looked past her at the car in the driveway. "Your *friend* isn't coming in?"

Kenzi met her father's eyes with a boldness that was new to her. "I asked him to give me a few minutes to speak with everyone first."

Dale closed the door. When he opened his mouth to say something, Kenzi cut him off. "Before you say anything, Dad, I want you to know that everything I need to say will be said respectfully. I love you and Mom, but some things need to change for me. I need to trust that everyone will show Dax the respect he has earned by being a good friend to me. I won't bring him in here if anyone is going to threaten him or throw little jabs at him. He's important to me." Kenzi took a deep breath. "And before you warn me not to upset Mom, I need you to know that I would never do anything to hurt her, but when I don't feel like I can be myself around her, it hurts both of us. She's your wife, but she's my mother, and I deserve the right to work out issues *with* her—not *through* you."

Dale studied Kenzi's face for a moment. "Grant and Lance are here. Asher, Emily, and Ian are on their way. Dax shouldn't be left in the car like that. I'll talk to him while you talk to everyone else."

Kenzi halted him with a hand on his arm. "Dad, don't—"

Dale placed his hand over hers. "Kenzi, I heard what you said last night and right now. I trust you to work things out with your mother in a way that she can handle it. Trust me with the man you love."

"I don't—" Kenzi didn't finish the lie. She did. She may not want to say the words out loud yet, but she took a page out of Dax's honesty book. "Dad, what Dax says when he's cornered doesn't represent how he has been with me. He could have come in here and been offended by what you know my brothers will say to him. He could have come looking for a fight or not come at all. He's sitting in the car because he didn't have a good relationship with his family, and he wants me to have one with mine. That's love, Dad. I don't care what he calls it."

Dale leaned forward and gave his daughter a kiss on the forehead. "No man is ever good enough for a father to imagine with his little girl, but Dax is close. I'd say he loves you as much as he can love anyone. I hope it's enough."

Kenzi clung to her father's arm a moment longer. "I'm willing to take that chance."

"Go see your mother, Kenzi. I'll be outside."

Kenzi watched her father close the door behind him as he left, and she prayed she'd made the right decision. Her father didn't have a cruel or vindictive bone in his body. Their past problems had stemmed from how protective he was with her mother, not because he'd ever wanted to hurt his children. He'd asked Kenzi to trust him with Dax, and Kenzi wanted to give him a chance to show he'd heard her. Really heard her.

She walked into the sitting room where her mother and two of her brothers were sitting. They all stood when she walked in.

Sophie said, "Kenzi, did you come alone? What happened? Boys, could you give me a moment alone with Kenzi?"

Kenzi raised a hand to stop them from leaving. "Wait. I need to say something first. Dax Marshall is here, but he's outside. Before you say anything to him I want you to know that I've never been happier than I am with him. I know you want to protect me, and that's why you test the men I date, but that will not happen this time. He is important to me. You don't need to know more than that about him." It was hard to decide which of the three looked more surprised by her strong words. "Any lack of respect you show him is a lack of respect you show me. Please keep that in mind when you speak to him." Kenzi lowered her hand and let out a shaky breath. "That's it. I just had to get that out."

Sophie looked on with her hands clasped in front of her.

Lance walked over and gave her a brief hug. "Dax may have a reputation for being an—" he stopped speaking abruptly, "but it's obvious that he has been good for you."

"Lance, your language," Sophie reprimanded.

"I didn't actually say it," Lance said, looking like a boy caught with his hand in a cookie jar.

Behind him, Grant shook his head. "I'll keep Lance in check."

Kenzi stepped toward her older brother and put her hands on her hips. The conversation had gone so much better than she'd hoped. She felt good enough to tease, "Him? Do you know how many men you've scared off by grilling them about how diversified their investment portfolios were? You're just as bad."

Lance chuckled. "See, Grant, it's not just me. He thinks he's perfect. I've tried to break it to him for years that I'm your favorite brother."

Kenzi shook her head in reluctant amusement. "I love you both the same, but I will kick your asses if you scare this one off."

"Kenzi," Sophie said automatically, but then smiled. "I can't wait to meet this Dax of yours. He sounds incredible."

"He is," Kenzi said. Originally she'd thought she needed to speak to her mother alone, but they could all benefit from what she wanted to say. "Dax told me a story about his family, and it really touched me. It made me not only appreciate all of you more, but it also showed me how I needed to change."

They all sat down and Kenzi told them about how Dax had been raised. She told them about his father and then his uncle. Although it wasn't really her story to tell, she felt it was important for them to hear because it would help them understand what she wanted and why Dax was so important to her. "Mom, I felt awful about what I said to you a few weeks ago. It was the truth, but it came out all wrong. I was dealing with things that had happened in my past."

Sophie moved to sit beside her daughter. Her expression was tormented. "You don't have to apologize, honey. I understand now. I feel so guilty that I didn't know. None of us knew."

There was so much that Kenzi could have said at that moment, but much of it wasn't important any longer. This wasn't about who had been right or wrong. This was about finding a way to move on together and do it in a healthier way. "I didn't know how to tell you, Mom." She looked around at her brothers. "I didn't know how to tell anyone. Dax helped me find my voice, and it's because of him that I found the courage to talk about what had happened to me. I'm making some big changes in my life, good changes, that I want all of you to be a part of. At first you might see me doing something and think that it's out of character for me, but it isn't. I've simply found the courage to be myself. I'll still come to you for advice, but when it comes to how I live my life, I'll be making those decisions now. So, like it or not, this is me."

Her mother gave her lap a pat. "If you're happy, we're

happy, Kenzi."

Kenzi smiled because she knew her mother meant it. She looked from one brother to the other and waited. They both nodded. The sound of the door opening was followed by Ian walking into the sitting room. He took in the mood and grimaced. "What did I miss?"

Lance stood and stretched. "Kenzi was warning us all to be on our best behavior with her boyfriend."

Sophie stood and crossed the room to give Ian a kiss. "He sounds lovely, so I'm sure we won't have a problem with that."

Ian frowned. "Are we talking about Dax Marshall? The same man who—"

Grant stepped closer to Ian. "We'll catch you up later. It's important to Kenzi that we're all nice to him."

Ian turned to Kenzi. They hadn't seen each other since she'd spoken at the high school. Due to how public opinion affected votes, Ian was the first to resent Barrington dirty laundry hitting the papers. Kenzi stood and faced him. She hoped telling her story hadn't affected him, but even if it had, she was speaking out about it. Even if he couldn't understand that at first, she had to trust that he soon would.

Ian walked over and pulled her unexpectedly into a tight hug. He didn't say anything, just kept hugging her. When he released her, he said, "Where's Asher?"

Sophie said, "He and Emily were running late. They had an appointment. My guess is Emily is pregnant. I wouldn't be surprised to hear that they're moving their wedding date up."

Jaws dropped open and all eyes in the room flew to her. Sophie adjusted her hair. "Don't look so shocked. Do I need to explain the birds and bees to you again?"

"God, no." Lance shuddered.

"Please don't," Grant said quickly.

Ian turned to Kenzi. "So, Kenzi, what do you want me to know about Dax?"

Even though she doubted Ian actually wanted the answer, she took her seat again and embraced her vow to be honest with her family. "I love him."

Just then Dale walked back into the room with Dax. Taffy was tucked beneath one of Dax's arms, her bandaged paw resting on his forearm. Dale said, "Asher called and said they're running late."

Kenzi jumped to her feet and searched Dax's face for any reaction to what she'd said. He might not have heard her. His protective wall was firmly in place, but Kenzi didn't know if that was in response to what she'd said or to the situation he was walking into.

Kenzi went to stand beside him. He handed Taffy to her. She hugged the dog gently and looked up into his eyes. He stared back at her, giving nothing away, but his expression was tense and cold. She wanted to shake him, ask him if he'd heard, but they weren't alone.

How ironic would it be if after warning my whole family not to scare him off—I did?

DAX REMAINED OUTWARDLY calm even as chaos broke loose inside him. *Kenzi loves me? She can't. She doesn't know me.*

She thinks she does because she met me during a rough time in her life.

Love? I said I wouldn't hurt her, but if she loves me, there's no good way this can end. He didn't have one good memory associated with the word.

Kenzi's mother cooed and seemed excited to meet Taffy. Kenzi left his side to show the dog to Sophie.

Dale started introducing Dax to his sons. Dax shook their hands on autopilot, but his mind was still racing. Before coming inside he'd had a polite but strained conversation with Dale. Although Dale hadn't apologized for anything he'd said the night before, he seemed sincere enough in his welcome. They'd carefully talked about nothing of importance until Dale had suggested Dax follow him in.

While talking to her mother, Kenzi looked up and gave him such a sweet look of concern Dax felt like even more of an ass. Had he been the kind of man to retreat, he would have stepped backward out of the room, out of Kenzi's life. Seeing her with her family brought home to him how very different they were.

Ian cleared his throat loudly and sounded as if he were repeating a question for a second time. "How long will you be in town?"

Dax forced his attention to the four men in front of him. "I haven't decided."

"You're based in London for the most part, is that correct?" Ian asked.

"That's correct."

"Was it business that brought you to town?"

Dale interjected, "Ian, go easy."

"Dad, you might be fooled by his puppy-holding act, but I know too much about Mr. Marshall to believe he's here just because he likes Kenzi. So, what is it, Marshall? Are you expanding your net beyond Poly-Shyn? Are you hoping that dating Kenzi will provide you with some kind of protection? It won't. In fact, it will have the opposite effect."

Dax took a deep breath. Ian was pushing him, but Dax had his temper firmly in check.

Lance nodded toward the door. "Ian, can we talk? Alone."

Grant put his hand on Ian's shoulder and said, "This is what happens when you're late, Ian. You missed an important memo. We'll be right back." With that, Grant and Lance escorted Ian into the hallway.

Dale said, "They mean well. They love their sister, and they only want the best for her."

Dale's explanation made him feel worse instead of better. He had no time to reflect on it, though, before Sophie and Kenzi walked over.

Sophie held out her hand. "So this is the infamous Dax Marshall."

Dax shook her hand gently. "Most people just call me Dax."

Sophie nodded. "Kenzi told me Taffy was a gift from you."

Dax met Kenzi's eyes briefly before confirming, "She was."

Sophie smiled. "You can tell a lot about a man by how he is with children and animals."

Dax shrugged. "I have next to no experience with either."

Sophie looked at her husband warmly. "My husband was pretty much the same. Dale, when we were dating, did you ever think you'd have six children?"

Dax loosened the tie around his neck a smidge. He'd never imagined himself as a family man. Hell, he'd never been in a relationship that lasted longer than a month. He looked at Kenzi quickly. *Is that what you want? To be married with more children than we could remember the names of? I'm not that man, Kenzi.*

"Mom, stop." Kenzi's face went a delightful shade of pink.

Dale gave Dax a sympathetic pat on the back. "I could use some coffee, how about you, Dax?"

"Sounds good."

Kenzi joined Dax as they walked into the other room. In a lowered voice, she said, "Is this as bad as I said it could be? We can leave."

Dax shook his head once. He'd come because he'd felt it was important to Kenzi, and he cared about her. Yes, she'd said she loved him, but did that have to mean relationship Armageddon was looming? Other women had said they loved him. They hadn't been devastated when he'd moved on.

Had they?

Dax wasn't the type to look back. He plowed forward in business and in his personal life. Most opportunities, like most relationships, had a peak value that diminished over time. Decisive actions optimized profit as well as they kept relationships simple. That's why he was brutally honest. *I told Kenzi I don't do relationships. I told her I'm not the man she thinks I am.*

He took a seat beside her at a table set with coffee and pastries. Kenzi put Taffy on the floor beside her feet. Her parents sat across from them. Dax looked at Kenzi and found her watching him with that fucking trusting expression of hers. He wanted to slap his hands down on the table and yell, "Stop looking at me like that. When you do I feel badly about every relationship I ended without regard for how the woman felt, every company I bought out from beneath a family like yours. You make me want to confess to things I never considered wrong. Stop."

Because when you look at me like that, I hate who I am.

Kenzi's brothers took their seats around the table. Lance shot Kenzi a not-so-subtle thumbs up. Grant shook his head in amused disgust at Lance's lack of tack. Ian nodded in acknowledgement, but his expression was guarded as he looked at Dax.

It was obvious Kenzi had done exactly what he'd suggested she do; she'd had a talk with her brothers. Dax took Kenzi's hand in his and gave it a supportive squeeze. No matter how tangled up he was about himself, watching Kenzi stand up for herself was amazing. He wanted to leave her better than he'd found her. If their time together could somehow strengthen her bond with her family, then he'd have done something right with her. That had to count for something.

He thought over their last conversation about Dean. If he offered Dean advice on how to keep his company, he doubted there was a man at the table who wouldn't be suspicious of his motives. Hell, if their roles were reversed he wouldn't trust him either.

Kenzi and her family were joking about something, but Dax wasn't paying attention. He was deep in thought. Despite the issues they had, Kenzi's love for her family was as clear as their love for her. The bond between her parents was equally unsettling. They'd been together for thirty-plus years. They shouldn't look that happy with one another. The longest marriage his father had had was three years. His uncle had never married and had always called marriage legalized prostitution. Men gave up half of everything they owned for the dubious right to fuck a woman. According to his uncle, wealth was better than any marriage license; it ensured sex was always readily available without subscribing to the outdated practice of monogamy. Anyone who didn't see that was a fool destined to be disappointed every time, as Dax's father had been. Until now, Dax had agreed with his uncle.

Dale, however, didn't look disappointed. The warmth in his eyes as he listened to Sophie tell a story was real. As were the tender touches the couple exchanged.

"How did you two meet?" Ian asked.

Dax pulled himself back to the present. "Kenzi was staying at a resort I'd just purchased."

"The Atlantia?"

"Yes."

Kenzi's voice rose with wonder. "You own the Atlantia? I love that place. I've been going there for the past five years. Is that why you were there?"

Ian continued without giving Dax time to answer Kenzi. "Before you get too excited, Kenzi, your friend isn't known for buying anything he doesn't intend to flip for fast profit."

Dale frowned at his son. "That's enough, Ian."

"Is it, Dad? I know people who have had the misfortune of dealing with Marshall. Good people who didn't deserve to wake up and see everything they'd worked for taken away just like that." Ian snapped his fingers in the air. "There are businessmen and then there are sharks. Sharks don't care about the wreckage they leave in their wake, they go in for the kill, then they move on. I'm sorry, Kenzi. I can't pretend to like a man I have no respect for."

Kenzi snapped, "How is any of what you described different from what Asher does?"

Dax stood. He opened his mouth to say something then saw the distress in Kenzi's eyes and changed his mind. "Dale, Sophie, thank you for the coffee."

Dale stood. "You don't have to leave, Son."

"My presence is overshadowing the reason Kenzi came today." *So is the fact that I want to punch one of your sons.*

Kenzi picked up Taffy. "If you leave, Dax, I'm going with you."

Dax nodded curtly to the others who were also coming to their feet. He forced his features and his voice to remain calm. "Give us a moment." He stepped into the hallway with

Kenzi so their conversation couldn't be easily overheard. "Kenzi, you came here to talk to your mother because she's hurting just like you were. I'm distracting you from that."

"You're not."

Dax touched her cheek softly. "I am. Stay and talk to them."

Kenzi shook her head sadly. "It wasn't supposed to be like this, Dax. I talked to my brothers. I thought they understood."

"I told you about my job. What I do doesn't always make me the most popular person in the room. I'm used to it. Meeting your family was—interesting." He smiled. "They're still better than mine."

Kenzi looked up at him with her half bald dog in her arms, and Dax's heart did that crazy thudding that only happened around her. She went up onto her tiptoes and gave him a brief kiss that was so sweet he almost changed his mind about leaving without her. "Don't go, Dax."

He rested his forehead on hers. He wasn't a man who spent much time worrying about how others felt, but he wanted Kenzi to be happy so much it hurt. "If I stay this will be about me. It wasn't supposed to be. Organize a fundraiser with your mother. Tell your brothers off again. But don't do any of that because of me, do it because you want to. Call me later."

Chapter Thirteen

K ENZI HUGGED TAFFY to her chest. She wanted to run after Dax, but she didn't. He was right. The reason she'd planned the visit that day had been because her mother had learned about the talk she'd given to the students. Their mother-daughter relationship needed some repairing. Kenzi turned to face her brothers who had come to stand just inside the dining room door. *And I have a few things I need to say to you, too.*

Her father came to her side. "Is he gone?"

Kenzi nodded.

Sophie gave Ian a sad look. "Ian, this was important to Kenzi."

Looking non-apologetic, Ian said, "Kenzi, you don't need a man like that in your life."

Kenzi put Taffy down and waved her hand at Ian, advancing on him. "Ian, someday you'll bring someone home, and I hope to God we treat her better than you treated Dax. I came here today because I wanted to make sure Mom and the rest of you were okay about what I spoke about at the school."

Ian instantly deflated. "Kenzi, when I heard what had happened to you—"

Kenzi shook her head angrily. "Don't. I am so angry with you right now. I wanted to leave with Dax, but he thinks a family like ours is worth fighting for. Are we? I understand that you think you can treat me the way you do because I've let you dictate so much of my life. Well, I'm done. I deserve to be treated with respect. I deserve to be heard. And I should be able to bring home anyone I want and not be afraid that you will drive him away."

Sophie moved closer and put an arm around Kenzi. "Don't get yourself all upset, Kenzi."

Kenzi took her mother's hand in hers. "Please don't tell me how to behave, Mom. I love you, but I can't pretend to be perfect for you. I won't. I want you to know me, the real me."

A confused frown wrinkled her mother's forehead. "Of course I know you, I'm your mother."

Kenzi couldn't believe the conversation had gotten as far as it had without her father intervening. She met his eyes and realized he wasn't going to. *He heard me. He finally did.* "Mom, ever since we were little we didn't want to upset you. We knew how much Kent's death had hurt you. We wanted you to be happy, but trying to protect you built a wall between us. Between you and me, anyway. I didn't feel like I could tell you anything. All I could be was the perfect little daughter you thought I was. But that wasn't me. I've made some bad choices and pulled myself through some tough times. I did all that without you, Mom, because I thought you couldn't handle the truth. I want to be me, Mom. And I want to talk to you about what happened to my twin. I want to share everything with you like mothers and daughters do. Can we do that, Mom? Can we be ourselves? Can that be good enough?"

Sophie pulled her daughter to her for a long, tearful hug. "I didn't know you felt this way, Kenzi. I didn't know."

"I know, Mom."

"Don't ever think there is anything you can't tell me, baby. I love you."

"I love you, too." Kenzi clung to her mother and sought her father's eyes over her shoulder. Her father was blinking back tears. She looked past him to see her brothers' reactions, but they were no longer in the room.

Kenzi stepped back and wiped the tears from her face. It hadn't been an easy road home, but she felt like she was finally there.

Emily walked into the room and stopped as soon as she saw Kenzi's face. "Is everything okay? I'm sorry, I shouldn't intrude. I'll go back outside."

"No," Kenzi said, surprising herself. Everything she didn't like about Emily suddenly felt petty. It wasn't her fault Kenzi's relationship with her parents was strained. Emily had done nothing but encourage them to spend more time together. *She's going to be my sister-in-law soon—very soon if Mom is right and she's pregnant. I can continue to resent her, but then isn't the problem me?* "Stay, Emily. You're family."

"You don't know what it means to me to hear you say

that." A huge smile spread across Emily's face, and she wiped a tear from her own eye. Kenzi walked over and gave her a hug that Emily returned warmly. Kenzi knew Emily had endured many losses, but it wasn't until just then that she realized how hard that must have been for her. Kenzi and her brothers had issues they needed to resolve, but she still had them in her life. Emily was alone—at least she had been before Asher had brought her home.

Taffy whined and Kenzi picked her back up. "Emily, meet Taffy. She's had a rough time, but she's healing up fast."

Emily ran her hands over the dog lightly. "The poor thing. Did you get her from a shelter?"

"Not exactly, she's a rescue though by every definition of the word." She briefly retold her story then said, "Now she's with me and is going to be spoiled rotten. I told her she'll have to find a way to pay it forward."

Emily tilted her head to one side and said, "I'd love to sculpt her. What do you think of a before and after work? It could be an exhibit at my museum and be lent out to others. It might be a nice way to get her story out there and help other rescues find homes."

What did I ever not like about her? "You'd do that?"

Sophie chimed in. "Line up all those projects for before the baby comes. No time for much after that."

"I'm sure," Emily said then her eyes rounded. "Wait, how do you know? We just found out today."

Sophie smiled up at her husband. He wrapped and arm around her, and they both said, "We're going to be grandparents."

Emily looked at the door then back to Kenzi. "We weren't going to say anything today."

Kenzi laughed. "We're all in trouble now, Mom. Unless you think we could pull off looking like we don't know when Asher finally tells us."

Dale looked around the room. "Where is Asher?

Emily motioned toward the door. "We met someone when we pulled in. Asher said he knew him. It sounded like they were headed for a heated business discussion, so I came in. Your brothers are out there with them, though. Who is that anyway?"

Kenzi's stomach flipped. With Taffy still in her arms she bolted for the door.

Dax.

She flew down the steps of her parents' house toward where Dax and her brothers were standing. Dax was on one side with Lance and Grant flanking him, looking as if they were trying to mediate. Ian was there, watching. Asher and Dax were facing off.

Asher growled, "Stay the fuck away from my sister."

"I'm not here for a fight, Asher," Dax said, but his tone implied that if one were coming his way he was ready for it.

Lance put a hand up in his oldest brother's direction. "Asher, Mom is in the house. Don't do this here."

Grant calmly agreed, "Let's all take this down a notch."

Asher shook his head in disgust. "Grant, you don't know this man as well as I do. If he's here it's because he has an agenda."

Dax's hands clenched, and his tone turned deadly cold. "This isn't about your sister, is it? You're scared. Rumor has it you're overextended from your last few projects. New Hampshire, wasn't it? Then trouble in Trundaie. No wonder you're nervous. If your investors start thinking you're indecisive, it could leave your company—vulnerable."

Asher lunged for Dax at the same time that Kenzi threw herself between them. The force behind Asher's move sent Kenzi falling backward with Taffy in her arms. She used her body to protect Taffy's and took the full impact of the driveway on her shoulder and the side of her head.

For a moment everything went still. There was no pain, no sound, just the shock of it and fear when Taffy bounced out of her arms. She pushed herself up and fell back against the tar as pain ricocheted through her head. She brought her hand to the side of her head and recoiled from the wetness she found there. She held a hand up to her face and almost passed out from the sight of her own blood.

A PIECE OF Dax died when he saw Kenzi hit the ground. He cursed himself for not catching her, for allowing himself to lose his temper with her brothers. He and Asher had clashed over business in the past, but never over anything personal. Although he knew Asher hadn't meant to hurt Kenzi, Dax could have killed him for it just then. Dax and Asher rushed to Kenzi's side, but Dale was already kneeling beside her.

Kenzi was trying to sit up again, but Dale asked her to stay still until he could see how badly she was hurt.

Sophie dropped down onto her knees beside Kenzi.

"Dale, she's bleeding."

Kenzi blinked several times. "I'm okay, Mom."

"No, you're not," Dale said and stood up. He pointed to Lance. "Call an ambulance. I want to have her looked at."

"Is Taffy all right?" Kenzi asked. Her words slurred slightly.

Emily bent down with Taffy in her arms. "She's right here. I have her. Don't worry. She's fine."

Asher said, "Kenzi, I didn't mean . . ."

Dax shed his coat, rolled it up, and handed it to Dale who placed it beneath Kenzi's head as a cushion. "Kenzi, I shouldn't have . . ."

Ian chimed in, "I think you've done enough damage for one day, Dax, don't you?"

Dale backed them up with an authority that silenced them. "Stop. All of you." He looked over each of the men gathered around Kenzi. "All of you should be ashamed of yourselves for acting the way you did today. You're grown men, for God's sake, not boys fighting in a school yard."

In all of Dax's life he couldn't remember ever feeling so badly about something he'd done. If he had held his tongue and walked away, Kenzi wouldn't be lying on the ground. *Do I require more evidence that I don't belong in her life? One day with her family, and we're in a bloody brawl.* He stepped toward her, feeling about as low as any man could. "Kenzi—"

"Not now," Dale said forcefully. "First, we're going to make sure Kenzi is okay. Then you can all apologize to her."

Asher opened his mouth to say something, but Dale spoke before him. "We're all going over to the hospital together, and everyone will be on their best behavior. Is that understood?"

Kenzi's brothers nodded.

Dale met Dax's eyes. "Whatever our differences are, they can wait until we know that Kenzi is okay."

Dax nodded in agreement. There was something about Dale that didn't leave an option for much else. His strength didn't come from brute force; it came from a moral rightness that couldn't be argued.

"Dax?" Kenzi called out.

Dale looked down at his daughter then back at Dax again. He moved out of the way, and Dax dropped to kneel beside Kenzi. He lightly touched one side of her face. He'd never been so angry, so scared, so sorry. "How do you feel?"

Kenzi's voice was shaky. "Like I tangled with the driveway, and it kicked my ass." She held her hand out to him, and he took it in his. "You look as bad as I feel."

Dax swallowed hard. "When I saw you falling—"

"I'll be fine. I have a hard head."

Dax took her hand and held it to the side of his face. "I shouldn't have come here today, Kenzi. This is my fault."

Kenzi gave his hand a squeeze. "You came for me, Dax. You couldn't have known any of this would happen. It was my fault."

"No, it—" Dax stopped talking when Kenzi closed her eyes and her face contorted with pain. He looked around until he spotted Lance. "Where is that ambulance?"

"Two minutes," Lance said, stepping toward them with a towel for Kenzi's head. "They said we shouldn't move her."

Sophie spoke up from the other side of Kenzi. "Dax, we saw what happened. It was no one's fault."

A siren announced the arrival of the ambulance. Emergency medical techs asked to be given room while they looked Kenzi over.

Dax reluctantly stepped back. He didn't want to leave her side, but he also didn't want to impede them from helping her. They applied a bandage and concluded she was sufficiently injured to warrant a few stitches and further testing to make sure she wasn't seriously hurt. Dax hardly breathed at all while they put a neck brace on her then moved her onto a gurney. They were pushing her past him when her hand reached out and grabbed his arm.

"Dax?" She looked confused and scared.

Sophie placed a hand on his other arm. "Why don't you ride with her, Dax? We'll meet you at the hospital."

Dax leaned over Kenzi. "Is that what you want, Kenzi?"

She nodded and closed her eyes, and a tear slid down her cheek. An army of men couldn't have pried him from her side after that. He released her hand only long enough for the EMTs to move her into the ambulance. Then he took his place by her side, careful to stay out of the way of the men who were placing monitors on her, but close enough to once again take her hand in his.

He spoke to her softly for the entire ride to the hospital. Under oath, he couldn't have remembered what he talked about. He talked about anything that came to mind because the sound of his voice seemed to soothe Kenzi.

Upon arrival at the hospital, he was asked once if he was

family. Without hesitation Dax said he was. He wasn't asked twice. He quickly realized that the lack of resistance had nothing to do with him. Kenzi was ushered into a private room rather than the usual emergency area. A doctor and a couple nurses were already waiting for her. Someone had called ahead.

Kenzi was quickly evaluated and a CT scan was ordered.

In a blink of an eye, Dale and Sophie were in the room with Dax and Kenzi. Dale spoke to the doctor while Sophie came over to check on Kenzi. Dax continued to hold Kenzi's hand even though part of him felt he should step aside for her mother. He looked at Sophie, feeling conflicted.

Sophie took his other hand in hers. "I understand now what Kenzi sees in you."

Dax looked down at Sophie's hand in his. He couldn't remember his own mother, and none of the women his father had married had been the nurturing type. Sophie had Kenzi's eyes, and in that moment she was looking at him with the same trusting, grateful expression he never felt worthy of. He didn't know what to say, so he said nothing. He simply held Sophie's hand while continuing to hold Kenzi's.

Kenzi was removed for a few minutes for the scan. Dale and Sophie stepped out of the room to speak with their sons who were waiting in a nearby family lounge. Dax moved to the window and looked out over the hospital parking lot, telling himself that Kenzi was already being cared for by the best doctors money could pay for. All he could do was wait.

Dale returned before anyone else. He walked over to

stand beside Dax and said, "I want to like you, Dax."

Dax fisted the hand he had resting on the window frame.

Dale continued, "When I spoke to you last night, I was angry. I've heard your name often recently and always linked to something I didn't approve of."

"That's a reaction I'm used to."

Dale was quiet for a moment. "I'm trying to figure you out. On one hand you have a solid reputation for being a bastard when it comes to business."

Dax turned his attention back out the window. If Dale wanted to beat him up he'd have to get in line. Dax was already doing a good job on himself. He knew he should have stayed away from Kenzi. Clay had said it the first time he'd met her, but Dax hadn't been able to. He'd told himself she needed him. If his only reason for being with her had truly been to help her, he wouldn't have slept with her.

Dale added, "On the other hand you've been kind to my daughter, and it's obvious that you care about her."

"I do," Dax said simply.

"Last night you said love wasn't in your vocabulary."

"I meant it."

"Tell me, what do you think love is, son?"

Dax shook his head in disgust. "A myth. My father loved many women. My uncle loved none." Mostly due to the anger he felt toward himself, Dax lashed out verbally. "You say you love your wife, but wasn't infidelity the reason your political career ended?"

Dale's harshly indrawn breath was the only sound in the room for a moment. "I haven't looked at another woman since I met Sophie. She's everything to me."

"I find that hard to believe. I've read the reports."

Dale's face tightened with anger. "The reports were manufactured."

"If there was no truth to it, why didn't you fight it?"

Dale was silent for a few minutes, then he said, "When you love a woman, truly love her, her happiness is more important than what anyone thinks of you. Sophie knows the truth, and she knows why I ended my career. Her opinion is the only one that matters to me. Not the public's. Not yours." He ran a hand through his hair. "Love isn't a myth, but it's also not the fairy tale people make it out to be in movies. It's a decision you make to put someone else's happiness before your own and to commit to something no matter what life throws at you. I don't know if you're the right man for my daughter or not, but I do know that you don't want to see her hurt any more than I do. My daughter's already falling in love with you, Dax. If you think you can love her back, you will always be welcome in my home. If you think you can't, end it now before she gets more attached to you than she already is."

"It's not that simple. If I could be the man Kenzi needs, I would be."

Dale gave him a pat on the shoulder. "I raised five sons, and they're still a work in progress. Don't give up on yourself yet." He sighed. "If I could impart one additional piece of advice: In life you'll have friends and enemies; be wise enough to know the difference and treat each accordingly."

Kenzi was wheeled back into the room. This time, Sophie, all her sons, and Emily accompanied them. The doctor explained that Kenzi had suffered a light concussion. Her head wound required only a couple of stitches and wasn't nearly as bad as the blood had made it look. He suggested she stay with someone that night who could watch over her.

Sophie was at Kenzi's side. "Come home with us, honey, at least until the doctor says you can be on your own."

Kenzi looked around the room for Dax. She didn't ask him to watch over her, but Dax knew she wanted to.

He thought about what her father had said, and he held himself back from offering. Her family was gathered around her. She'd been worried about the relationship with her mother, afraid it was broken beyond repair. But she was by her side. Kenzi was where she needed to be.

Dax bent and kissed Kenzi on the cheek. "I'll call you tonight."

She held onto his arm for a moment then released it. There were too many people in the room for either of them to say much. "I don't know where my cell phone is."

Grant said, "We have all your things, Kenzi."

Emily stepped forward. "Taffy is still at your parents' house. I can pick up food for her if you tell me a brand."

Willa and Lexi burst into the room. "Kenzi, are you okay? What happened?" they asked in unison.

Kenzi was completely preoccupied answering questions. Dax excused himself from the room. He looked at each of her brothers as he walked past them. Lance and Grant looked somber. Ian was carefully neutral, and Asher looked as if he wanted to finish what they'd started earlier.

Dale was right about one thing, though, their opinions didn't matter much to Dax. Kenzi would be happy they were there, and that's what was important.

Once outside, Dax called for his town car. He went to his office and told his secretary he didn't want to be disturbed. With a bottle of Jack Daniels in one hand and a glass in the other, Dax sank into one of the chairs.

He poured himself a generous shot, downed it, then poured himself another. The door of his office opened and Kate popped her head in. "I know you told me you didn't want to be disturbed, but Mr. Landon is on the phone. He said he's been trying to call you."

"What part of 'hold my calls' is fucking confusing?" Dax snapped and waved for Kate to close the door.

Kate closed the door hastily which made Dax feel even more like a bastard.

If that were possible.

Chapter Fourteen

LATER THAT NIGHT Kenzi rolled over in bed, groaned as the move made her head throb again, and turned on a lamp so she could see the clock on her nightstand. *Nine o'clock. Dax isn't going to call.*

Can I even blame him?

It was impossible to be angry with him after all he'd done for her. The more Kenzi replayed the last two days in her head, the more she wondered if she'd ever see him again.

The sex had been amazing, but a man like Dax could probably find a hundred women willing to jump in bed with him who were just as enthusiastic about being with him as she'd been.

Did he hear me say I love him? I hope not. That's the only way this could be worse.

Dax had been clear about his opinion of love. She'd gotten to know him well enough to understand why he felt that way. No one had ever shown Dax how to love.

Foolish me, thinking I could.

All I did by saying it was pressure him then toss him to the wolves.

Being with Dax had brought about so many good changes within Kenzi she'd started to think anything was possible. *Like my brothers respecting my wishes.*

I shouldn't have brought Dax home. I shouldn't have exposed him to them. I knew they would find a way to drive him away. Who can blame a man for not wanting a repeat of today?

Taffy whined for Kenzi from her bed on the floor. Kenzi rolled onto her stomach near the edge and dropped a hand to pet the dog's head. "I want to call him so badly, but that wouldn't be fair to him. He'd talk to me. He might even come over if I asked him to, but I don't want him to be with me because I asked him to. That's probably the one thing that would hurt more than not seeing him at all—knowing he was with me out of pity."

A light knock on the door was followed by Sophie entering the room. "How do you feel?"

"Not so good," Kenzi answered honestly then regretted it when her mother rushed to her bedside.

"The doctor said it was fine for you to sleep unless you develop any other symptoms. What's wrong?"

Kenzi sat up slowly. "I'm fine, Mom. It's not my head that hurts."

"Oh," Sophie said and sat on the edge of the bed. "You didn't hear from your friend?"

"No, and could I really blame him if he never calls again?"

Sophie tucked a loose lock of hair behind Kenzi's ear. "He'll call."

"I don't know, Mom. Do you know how many of my

boyfriends tend to call after meeting my brothers? Zip. Zero. Zilch. The Barringtons have a one hundred percent winning streak when it comes to destroying my love life."

Sophie rubbed Kenzi's arm sympathetically. "Dax isn't like those other men. You'll see."

Kenzi looked away. "You don't understand. How could you? Dad never had to deal with anyone like Asher."

"He had worse, Kenzi. Much worse."

Kenzi turned and met her mother's eyes. "Your father?"

Sophie shook her head sadly. "My sister, Patrice. Your brothers love you, and they may not express it well, but they want the best for you. My sister didn't love anyone. She was jealous and vindictive. She married a man she didn't love and hated that I had your father. We both had children, and I celebrated the birth of each of hers, but she couldn't do the same when all of you were born. Your birth in particular was more than she could handle. She'd always wanted a girl and there you were, my little angel. She resented you so much she couldn't be there for me when I fell into a depression over losing Kent. All she could see was I had something she didn't. Soon after that, she started a rumor about your father cheating on me. I didn't believe it, but the press did. False proof came to us in the mail, showing he'd used public monies to support his mistress. The sender threatened to release the proof to the public if your father didn't resign. It was an ugly lie that we traced back to my sister."

"Oh, my God, Mom. Couldn't you fight it? I mean, if you knew it was her, how could you let her do that?"

Sophie smoothed the material of her skirt. "I was scared.

My family was extremely wealthy, and I was afraid I wouldn't be able to protect your father if they came for him. I begged him not to take my sister on. I knew if he did she was capable of anything. So, your father resigned and let her win. It's not something I'm very proud of. Your father gave up everything for me. He never complained, never spoke badly of my family. When Dale resigned, I felt guilty that I hadn't done more to protect him. I've regretted it every day since. When I saw you run to protect Dax from Asher I was so proud of you. I was terrified when you went flying but also proud that you're stronger than I was. If I were given a second chance to defend your father I'd like to think I'd be more like you."

Kenzi hugged her mother and rested her cheek on her shoulder. "Well that explains why you never talk about your family."

Her mother rubbed her back gently. "Asher didn't mean to hurt you, Kenzi, but he was wrong to treat Dax the way he did. He's downstairs along with the rest of your brothers. If you're up to it, you should talk to him. I moved away from my sister rather than face our problems head-on, and it only made things worse. Tell him you're angry with him. Make it clear to him that he can't treat your friends that way. Then tell him you love him because at the end of the day he's your brother, and I want more for both of you than I had with my sister."

Kenzi raised her head. "Now you sound like Dax."

Sophie smiled. "I knew there was a reason I liked him. He reminds me of your father in some ways. The way he watches you when you talk. The way he smiles when you smile. He may not have the words to express it, Kenzi, but he loves you."

I want to believe that. I so desperately want that to be true.

Kenzi took a deep breath and moved backward to rest against the headboard of her bed. She arranged the bed sheets at her waist. "Mom, please tell Asher I'd like to speak with him."

Sophie stood. She paused at the door before opening it. "Be kind but firm, Kenzi. Men are funny creatures. They're strong on the outside, but beneath all their talk, they're just as scared and easily hurt as we are. You can be right and still lose if your talk pushes you farther away from each other."

"I think I understand, Mom."

Sophie opened the door. "Don't go too easy on him."

"Okay. Okay."

Sophie nodded. "I'll tell him to come up."

"Mom," Kenzi called out.

Her mother turned. "Yes, honey?"

"I feel like you see me now, really see me."

"Oh, honey. I'm so sorry—"

"No, please don't. Don't apologize. I'm trying to tell you that, beyond everything else, I'm grateful for this: you and me. This is what I've wanted for so long. I love you, Mom."

"I love you, too, honey." Sophie smiled with tears in her eyes, then she left to get Asher.

ACROSS TOWN DAX was wishing he'd gone for a run instead of drinking. He felt trapped in his office, trapped in his own head. He'd taken out his cellphone countless times to call Kenzi then put it back on the arm of the chair.

He rested the half bottle of liquor on one knee and his empty glass on his other. He'd hoped a few shots would stop his thoughts from circling back to the moment he'd watched in horror as Kenzi's head hit the tar of the driveway. She'd lain there motionless for what had felt like an eternity. He wasn't a man who was used to feeling afraid, but fear had seared through him and left him shaken.

He couldn't stop thinking about what Dale had said to him at the hospital. *If I can't love his daughter, I should leave now before she gets more attached.*

Kenzi, I want to love you.

The door to his office opened. Clay strolled in and took the seat across from him. "You know what's scarier than having someone like you for a boss? Watching someone like you get shitfaced alone in their office. Kate's a wreck out there."

"What I do is none of her business—or yours."

He leaned forward and assessed Dax's condition. "How drunk are you?"

"Not enough," Dax growled.

Clay snatched the phone from beside Dax and slipped it into the breast pocket of his jacket. "You'll thank me later."

Dax groaned and laid his head back. "You're a good friend, Clay. I don't know if I've ever told you that, but you are."

Clay removed the bottle and the glass from Dax's hand. "You've had more than enough."

Dax opened his eyes. "I'm a complete asshole. Why are you my friend?"

Clay made a pained face. "You won't even remember this tomorrow. Why don't I have Kate get us some coffee?"

Dax slammed his hand down on the arm of his chair. "I'm serious. Do I have one goddamned redeeming quality? Outside of knowing how to make money?"

Clay sat back and steepled his fingers in thought. "I never wonder what you're thinking. There are a lot of fake people in the world, but you're not one of them. If you say something you mean it."

Dax narrowed his eyes at the blurry image of his friend across from him. "I never saw the need to lie."

"I know. That's part of what makes you you. You don't give a shit what anyone thinks about you." When Dax didn't say anything, Clay leaned forward again. "Uh-oh. This is about Kenzi, isn't it? No one else gets to you like she does."

Dax rubbed his hand over his eyes. "I slept with her, Clay. And it was good. It was so fucking good. We—"

Clay laughed. "I'm positive you don't want me to know this. So you finally fucked her. Why are you wallowing in Jack Daniels instead of doing it again?"

Dax groaned. "I met her family."

"I did warn you that they wouldn't like you."

"They hate me."

"I told you they would."

"No, I mean they really fucking hate me. I thought we could keep it simple, but then she said she loved me, and her father wanted me to say something, and then I was holding her mother's hand, and Kenzi was hurt."

"You made a pass at Kenzi's mother?" Clay's eyebrows shot up.

As the alcohol seeped into his brain, Dax struggled to clarify. "No, Kenzi was bleeding. She jumped in front of her brother when he was coming for me. She hit her head."

"Holy shit, is she okay?"

"I think so. Concussion? Some stitches. I left her with her family at the hospital. I was supposed to call her, but I didn't. Her father told me to stay away if I can't love her." Dax pressed his lips together sadly. "I can't love anyone. You know me. I'm an asshole."

"I'm not sure you don't love her."

"What?"

"I'm no expert on love, but you're miserable, and I've never seen you like this. You should at least consider the possibility."

"Maybe. She has me thinking crazy things. Like I want to help the Hendersons keep their company. Dean is a fucking hero. He deserves to have something good come from this. What do you think of that? What if I helped someone keep something instead of helping them lose it?"

"I don't really understand why Dean is a hero, but that's definitely crazy."

"I know, right? I mean, can you imagine what he'd say if I told him I'd invest in his company? And not so I could buy it out?"

"Easy, there, Dax. Did you drink anything besides the Jack?"

Dax heard the slur in his own words, but as he shared the idea he found he liked it. "Do you believe people can change?"

"Why don't we talk about this when you're sober?"

"I should have called Kenzi."

"Call her tomorrow."

"She's waiting for my call now. What is she going to think if I don't call her? That I don't care that she was hurt?"

"Dax, you can't call her drunk."

"I'm not drunk."

"Really?"

Dax waved four fingers in front of his face. "I only had three . . . or six . . . maybe nine shots."

Clay stood. "Come on, let's get you out of here before anyone sees you like this."

Dax slept part of the drive back to his place. Clay guided him inside and to the door of his bedroom. "Go to bed, friend. I'll check on you tomorrow."

Dax walked over to his bed and dropped onto it face first. "I'm fine."

Clay put Dax's phone on his nightstand. "Call me if you need me, but the best thing you can do is just sleep this off."

Dax rolled over onto his back. "When I'm with Kenzi, she's my redeeming quality."

Clay turned off the light. "Good talk. Night, Dax."

Dax's eyes closed briefly, and he imagined Kenzi. He remembered how she'd looked the first night he'd met her. He'd sensed a deep sadness in her. That memory morphed as images of them together flipped like a photo album in his head. He loved how she looked sitting across the table from him on a date. He loved how she looked in the morning, all rosy from a night of lovemaking. Her voice was the one he wanted to hear whenever his phone rang. She was the first person he wanted to see when he left work.

He reached for his cellphone and found her number then pressed call. Her phone went to messages. He groaned and said, "Kenzi, I hope you're okay. I'm so miserable . . . Clay thinks this is love. Goodnight."

He hung up, tossed his phone onto the floor and passed out.

Chapter Fifteen

KENZI WAS DRESSED and dabbing her stitches with the medicine her doctor had sent home. Her cut was small and almost hadn't required stitches, but since it would be covered by hair she had the option of shaving a larger area for a bandage to attach to or a smaller one and having it stitched then keeping it clean.

Her head was still a little sore, but the doctor had told her to expect that. He'd suggested she not take pain medication if she didn't need to, and Kenzi was glad she hadn't. She was already feeling emotional and tired without adding another layer to it.

Her talk with Asher had ended on a good note, but there had been some moments that Kenzi hadn't been sure it would. Asher had come ready to apologize for hurting her. When he'd realized it wasn't her injury that she was upset about, he'd become defensive.

He'd tried to tell her that Dax played just above the letter of the law. "He is conscienceless. All he cares about is money. He's a self-absorbed egotist."

Kenzi had asked, "So how is he different than you?"

That had temporarily stumped Asher. He'd run a hand through his hair in frustration. "I'm your brother. I can't sit back and watch someone like him use you."

Kenzi clasped her hands in front of her. "You might not like Dax, but I do. He's been good to me—for me. He came here yesterday because he knew I was nervous about facing Mom after my story went public. When you hurt him, you hurt me." Kenzi had cleared her throat. "If he ever does come around again, please remember that. You say you love me; well, prove it. You don't have to care about everyone I do, but how would you feel if I insulted Emily?"

Asher had frowned. "It's not the same thing at all."

"That's where you're wrong, Asher. It's exactly the same. That's how you hurt me tonight, not by pushing me to the ground."

"Dax is . . ." Asher stopped and rubbed his chin. "Be careful, Kenzi. That's all."

"I will be."

Asher had hugged her and said he'd check on her the next day. Kenzi had turned off her light and hugged a pillow to her, wishing it were Dax.

Now, as she applied the last of her makeup, she told herself to be strong. Dax would call her. Or he wouldn't. She had to find a way to be okay with either outcome.

Kenzi picked her phone off the nightstand and checked it then swore when she saw that the battery had drained to zero. She plugged it in and waited, hating how desperately she wanted to see a text or voice message from Dax. She warned herself that there might not be one.

The phone turned on and the beep announcing a waiting message was the sweetest sound Kenzi had ever heard. She scrolled to her messages and held her breath when she saw that she had one from Dax.

She listened to the message once, then again. She picked up the house phone in her room and called Willa and Lexi. After assuring both of them she was fine, she asked them if they could listen to something and give their opinion.

"Is that Dax?" Willa asked.

"Of course that's Dax," Lexi said sarcastically. "Who else do you think it would be?"

"He sounds drunk," Kenzi said, biting her bottom lip in indecision.

"Never drunk call anyone. Even Lexi knows that."

Lexi parried back, "What does that mean, *even I know that*?"

Willa said, "Don't get all sensitive, Lexi. This is about Kenzi."

"Oh, we will circle back to this later," Lexi said. "Can you play his message again?"

Kenzi did. "Did he just say he loves me?"

"It does sound that way," Willa said slowly.

"He's crazy about you," Lexi said.

"No," Willa corrected. "We don't know that for sure. What does he say when he's sober?"

"He says he doesn't believe in love."

Lexi snorted. "That's what guys say when they're falling hard."

"Or that's how he actually feels, and it was the alcohol

talking. The last time you got drunk, Lexi, you kept hugging the pizza delivery man. All because he remembered the pepperonis. I had to peel you off him. Poor guy was devastated when he came back a week later and you didn't even get off the couch."

"No, he thought you were me, remember? That's why I stopped thinking he was so cute."

Kenzi sat on the edge of her bed. "Not to make this all about me, but could this be about me for a minute? Should I call him? What should I say?"

"He might not remember he called you," Lexi said with a gleeful laugh. "I've done that."

Ever the voice of reason, Willa said, "There are so many ways this could be awkward. What about calling him and just saying, 'Hey, I saw that you called. Did you want something?'"

Lexi said, "How is that not awkward? If he remembers the call, he's not proud of making it. If he doesn't remember it, she looks like an ass."

Kenzi brought a hand to her throbbing temple. "I don't know if I feel better or worse now."

Sophie walked in and sat beside her on the bed. "Is that the doctor?"

Kenzi shook her head and winced. "No, it's Lexi and Willa."

Sophie smiled. "Tell them I said hello."

Willa said, "Ask your mom what she'd do."

Even though Willa wasn't on speakerphone her voice carried. Sophie tilted her head to one side. "What I'd do about what?"

Kenzi decided if she and her mother were going to stay close she needed to know what was going on. "Dax called me." She played the message for Sophie.

Lexi said, "I'd pay a hundred dollars to see the expression on your mother's face."

Sophie chuckled. "I can hear you, dear."

"Oh, sorry," Lexi said and Willa laughed.

Kenzi placed the cellphone back on the nightstand. "I didn't get the message until this morning. We were discussing if I should call him and if I do what I should say. What do you think, Mom?"

"I don't think you've asked me about a boy since before—" Sophie stopped, looking horrified at what she'd almost said.

Kenzi hugged her. The past was losing its power to upset her. "Well, I'm asking now," she said gently. "What do you think I should do?"

Sophie's eyes misted up, and she took a moment to compose herself. "You should trust your heart, Kenzi. We've tried to protect you in the past, and we were wrong. You know Dax better than anyone. What do you think the message means?"

Still holding the house phone in one hand, Kenzi took her time responding. She let her mother's question echo through her until an answer came to her. "Dax had a tough childhood. He told me about how he never knew his mother and how no one stayed in his life for long. I think he doesn't want to need anyone because he doesn't want to get hurt again."

"That is so sad," Willa and Lexi said in unison.

Sophie squeezed one of Kenzi's hands. "So what will you do?"

Kenzi thought it over then said, "I'll give him time to realize he can't live without me. And when he comes back to me, I'm going to love him with all my heart. You taught me how to do that, Mom. You and Dad."

Sophie wiped away a tear and kissed Kenzi's cheek.

Kenzi's heart was bursting with love for her family, her friends, and for Dax. Regardless of how hard it would be to wait, Kenzi was no longer afraid. Dax had helped her find her way home. If he let her, she'd do the same for him.

DAX LEANED BACK in his office chair the next morning and closed his eyes. His head was pounding, and his stomach was churning. He'd tried to push himself through his email, but he wasn't having the most productive morning.

What the hell was I thinking, drinking here last night? Thank God Clay took me home before I made a fool of myself in front of my staff.

Not that anyone would have the nerve to mention it if he did, but he still preferred his staff to fear him rather than mock him at the water cooler.

He wasn't a big drinker so the shots had hit him hard. *At least I didn't throw up on anyone.* Dax smiled at the memory of how Kenzi had done just that and left an impression on him and his shoes.

Kate knocked on the door and popped her head in. "Mr.

Henderson is on hold on line one."

"Which Henderson?"

"He didn't say."

Dax rubbed his forehead and reached for his phone. "I'll take it." Kate closed the door as she left. "Marshall here."

"Marshall, it's Dean Henderson. I received a phone call from Clay Landon this morning. He said you wanted to speak to me. I told him there was nothing I could imagine you could say that I'd want to hear, but he assured me there was. What do you fucking want, Marshall?"

"You're going to lose Poly-Shyn."

"That's what this is about? I heard you'd changed your mind about trying for a buyout, but I didn't believe it. Looks like I was right. Threaten all you'd like, Marshall, you won't get Poly-Shyn."

Dax took a deep breath. *I'm going to kill you, Clay.* "I'm not threatening you. I'm considering investing in your company."

"Do you take me for a fool? I've seen your early-bird leveraged takeovers. We're ready for you."

"Pull your head out of your ass long enough to hear what I'm saying, Dean. I don't want your fucking company, but I wasn't the only one who was interested in it." Dale's words came back to him then: *In life you'll have friends and enemies; be wise enough to know the difference and treat each according- ly.* No matter how grating Dax found him, Dean had silenced someone who could have made Kenzi's life hell, and he'd kept Kenzi's secret. He might be a cocky little shit, but he wasn't an enemy. Now all Dax had to do was prove it to him. "I'll send you over a proposal. Read it. What you decide after that is your choice, but I'd like to see you save your father's company."

"Why?"

"Let's just say I'm diversifying my business approach."

"What the fuck does that mean?"

"It means I want to see if I am as good at saving a company as I am at dissolving one."

Chapter Sixteen

A WEEK LATER, Kenzi sat at the new desk she'd purchased for her apartment and opened her laptop. Her stitches were out, and she was feeling healthy and positive. She sifted through several requests from organizations looking for funding. She printed them out, placed them in folders, and stacked them on her desk. She and her mother had plans to spend the afternoon sorting through the requests and deciding how to move forward with helping as many as they could.

Kenzi had contacted the director she'd worked with at the high school and was relieved to hear that the girl she'd been concerned about was getting the resources she needed. Kenzi finally felt in control of her life and optimistic about her future.

Kenzi's cell phone rang. "Hello?"

"Hi, Kenzi. It's Emily. I'm almost finished with Taffy's first sculpture. Would you like to look at it and tell me what you think?"

"I'd love that," Kenzi said. "My mother is coming by this afternoon to help me organize some stuff. Is it at your apartment?"

"Yes, although now that I think about it, maybe I should bring it to you."

"I don't mind the trip."

"You've never seen my studio here, Kenzi. Your brother decorated it with, let's just say his sense of humor."

"Asher has a sense of humor? I need to see this."

Emily laughed nervously. "Could we rewind and pretend I never brought any of this up? I'm sure I shouldn't have. Besides, it'll all be put away in storage soon as it becomes the baby room."

With a huge smile Kenzi said, "You know curiosity is now going to make it impossible for me to stay out of that room."

Emily laughed again. "That's why I'll bring the sculpture to you. So, what time works? Four?"

"Four it is." After Kenzi hung up, she thought about how much she was enjoying her new friendship with Emily. She saw her in an entirely new light. At first Kenzi had thought it was Emily's kindness to Taffy that had won her over, but she saw now it was more than that.

Kenzi had spent a significant portion of her life focusing on what was wrong with her family, and that habit had extended to Emily. She and Emily had finally had a real talk and were getting to know each other.

It wasn't easy to admit to Emily that she'd felt threatened by her bond with her mother, but once addressed, it was no longer an issue. Emily, like Sophie, was a people pleaser. Kenzi, too. Lexi said that was the problem with too many nice chefs trying to share a kitchen, for something new to happen someone had to stir things up.

It was an interesting metaphor, but Kenzi understood what she meant. Her life had needed a little stirring up and honesty was the key ingredient necessary for that to happen. Healing hadn't been possible while all of them had worried more about hurting each other than working through their problems.

A commitment to facing problems rather than running from them was what was driving Kenzi to give back to her community. Yes, she'd been hurt, but there were people right now suffering in many different ways. She couldn't help all of them, but she was determined to make a difference.

Taffy was finally bandage-free, and Kenzi had already spoken to a woman about taking classes so she could be a volunteer dog, a mascot of sorts for shelters who wanted to highlight success stories. It wasn't clear if Taffy yet had the personality for it, but either way Kenzi felt the journey would be good for both of them.

It was with the same positive frame of mind that Kenzi was keeping her heart open to Dax, even though he hadn't contacted her since his drunken message. She told herself she would wait for him to work his feelings out, and so far she hadn't wavered. She didn't want to pressure him into something he wasn't ready for, nor did she want to chase him away. Waiting wasn't easy, but Dax had shown her time and time again that he heard her and cared about how she felt. This was her chance to show him that she heard him as well and valued his feelings.

It was a gamble. There was a chance that the more time they went without talking, the less likely it was she'd ever hear from him again. She shook her head to clear that negative thought.

Believing in anything is scary, but it is a whole lot less painful than believing in nothing.

DAX SLAMMED A drawer in his London office desk and stood. He'd returned to London to clear his head, but it wasn't proving to be as easy as that. The only thing he'd heard from Dean Henderson was that he needed more time to comb through his proposal.

Dax came back expecting his London team to be in disarray, but they were hitting their target goals, and that only irritated Dax more. He'd threaten to fire enough of them that Kate was presently running interference between him and his key people.

A week back in his normal routine should have been enough to shake him out of the foul mood that had descended upon him since he'd made up his mind to never see Kenzi again. No such luck.

No matter how he spun his time with Kenzi, he still hated himself for how it had played out. He'd met her during a time when she'd obviously been working through some painful memories. He'd taken advantage of that vulnerability and had sex with her even though he'd told himself he wouldn't. And to add insult to injury, or injury to injury, he'd gone with her to see her parents—an act that she had seen as evidence that he felt more for her than he did.

He'd lost his temper and, regardless of what Sophie had said about it being no one's fault, he held himself accountable for Kenzi getting hurt. He should have ended their friendship sooner. He should have followed Clay's advice and stayed away from her.

He'd picked up his phone several times a day over the last week and almost called her. He wanted to make sure she was okay. He wanted to explain that he'd never meant to hurt her. He didn't make the call, though, because her father had been right. If he couldn't love her, the kindest thing he could do was end it before she became even more attached to him.

Clay called and asked if he wanted to run a 10K run with him in Greece. Dax declined. He said he was too busy. It was the first lie he'd ever told Clay, but he didn't want to answer the questions his friend would ask if he told him the truth.

Dax didn't have the energy for a run like that. He hadn't slept well in over a week. He barely ate to the point where Kate had started ordering lunch for him. He felt like shit, and he knew he was beginning to look just as bad.

He told himself he'd probably caught something during his trip to the United States and was feeling drained as he fought it off. He refused to consider that how he felt was at all related to missing Kenzi.

Because he didn't.

He wouldn't allow himself to.

Cutting off all contact with her had been necessary and feeling one way or another about it would be a waste of emotion. Kenzi might be angry with him for not calling, but she'd soon see how it was for the best.

She'd move on, meet someone new, settle down with someone her family approved of, and have the children he knew she wanted. Dax punched the wooden cabinet door beside his desk and cursed as it fell to the floor.

Kate opened the door, took one look at Dax, and closed it hastily. He swore again and opened his office door.

"Go home, Kate."

She nodded and turned off her computer. "Mr. Marshall, will we be returning to the United States soon? My sister is planning a family reunion, and she asked if I'll be around. Since I go where you go, I wasn't sure what to tell her."

"I have no plans of returning to Boston any time soon. Whatever business we have with companies there can be conducted from here."

"Thank you, Mr. Marshall." Kate gathered up her purse and said, "I liked Boston. If you do decide to relocate there, I'll happily return with you. I could always fly back for the reunion."

"I have no reason to return to Boston," Dax said forcefully.

"Of course. See you tomorrow, Mr. Marshall," Kate said and ducked out.

Dax returned to his desk and spent the rest of the evening answering email. Normally his phone would have rung repeatedly with calls from his staff with either questions or updates. The silence was evidence that his staff was running scared. Productivity was up, which was the only good byproduct of an otherwise shitty week.

Chapter Seventeen

A COUPLE WEEKS later, Kenzi found herself enjoying an intense game of Scrabble with her family. Grant was winning, but Asher was about to jump to the lead with a very long, dubiously spelled word.

Lance took out his phone to confirm the spelling.

Ian assured his brothers that winning or losing the game wouldn't change history in any measurable way.

With humor twinkling in his eyes, Grant said, "That's what everyone says when they're down by so much that they can't win."

"Really? I have a Z right here and a plan for how to use it," Ian said.

Looking up from his phone, Lance said, "Did you know that there is a debate going on regarding changing the value of Z to six instead of ten points? Wow, these people are serious about their Scrabble. They have a whole rationale for why certain letters should be re-valued."

"Nothing is changing during this game," Ian said seriously enough that several of his brothers chuckled.

Sophie cut in, "Remember this is for fun, boys."

Asher raised an eyebrow at Ian and joked, "Unless you *lose*, and then who enjoys that?"

Ian threw a Scrabble tile at Asher.

Asher threw one back at him.

Via Skype, Andrew chimed in from Afghanistan, "It's all fun and games until someone loses an I."

A general groan was echoed at his play on words. "That was so bad, Andrew. So bad."

Lance found Asher's spelling of the word and tallied the score. "Asher is winning by two points." He looked over at Emily and Kenzi. "You know you can't combine your points, right? And the goal is to have the most." He ducked when Kenzi swatted at him. "Just making sure you understand the way this is played."

Emily put her hand on her stomach even though it was still flat. "I can't believe you would make fun of a pregnant woman. Don't you know our emotions are all over the place?"

Lance's mouth dropped open. He looked at Asher who nodded. Ian and Grant congratulated both Asher and Emily. Andrew made them promise to wait until he was back before birthing anything. Asher moved over to sit beside Emily, smiling with pride.

Kenzi winked at Emily. "Well played, Emily. Well played."

Emily smiled, looking around the table. "I guess now would also be a good time to tell you that we're moving our wedding date up."

"Really?" Sophie asked, raising her voice as if she were

surprised.

Kenzi coughed.

Asher put an arm around Emily's waist. "We've decided to keep it simple. We'd like to have it at our place in Nantucket in September. Nothing big. Just family and close friends."

Dale asked, "Are we inviting the Andrades? I feel like we should since they came out and supported Emily's museum."

Asher looked from his mother to Emily. "I'm leaving the wedding planning in Emily's hands."

"Smart man," Lance said dryly.

Emily took a moment to think about it then said, "They've been so kind to me. Sophie, they're your family. If you want them there, I think we should invite them."

Ian shook his head. "There goes your small wedding."

Dale put his hand on Sophie's. "The wedding itself doesn't matter. Who you choose to spend the rest of your life with does."

Had anyone else said it, one of the men in the room might have made a joke, but Dale spoke with such deep sincerity that his words were followed by a quiet moment of reflection. He was the first one to break the silence. "Your mother and I went to lunch with Brice Henderson. He said Dean is definitely taking over his family's company, and it looks like things might go well with that because Dax is helping him."

Kenzi's jaw dropped open. "Dax is helping Dean?"

"I don't know the details of it, but Dax sent Dean a proposal on how they could work together to save it." Dale nodded at his oldest son. "Asher, did you know about this?"

Asher nodded. "I didn't know what to think when I first heard, but it seems straightforward enough." He cleared his throat. "Marshall is willing to invest in Poly-Shyn and work with Dean to turn it around. I've known Dax for a long time, and I've never seen him help anyone."

Kenzi's heart started beating wildly in her chest. "He knows what Dean did for me."

Ian reached over and held Kenzi's hand. "I can't believe I'm going to say this, but we might have been wrong about him."

Asher shook his head slowly. "No, we've seen Marshall in action for a long time. People like that don't change."

Emily laid a hand on his cheek. "Unless they have a reason to. I remember a certain, let's say . . . arrogant man, who told me that winning was all that mattered to him. That's not what you say today. Is it impossible to imagine that meeting someone as amazing as your sister might change Dax's priorities, too?"

Kenzi waited and hid a smile. *You go Emily. You really are good for my brother.*

Asher looked across at his sister. "No, it's not impossible to imagine. I just don't want to be wrong about him. Have you even heard from him?"

Kenzi clasped her hands on her lap. "I haven't." She looked at her father. Her mind was racing. Dax was helping Dean? That had to be proof that he loved her. But, as Asher had pointed out, it wasn't enough for him to call her. "Dad, what do you think?"

Dale rubbed one of his temples in thought then said, "The night you were hurt, I had a conversation with Dax. I told him if he loved you he would always be welcome here, but if he couldn't he needed to stay away from you before you became even more attached to him."

"Dad," Kenzi said in horror, "that's why he didn't call."

Dale nodded. "Which I took as his answer, but if he's helping Dean because he knows you care about him, I don't know what I think anymore."

"I do," Sophie said softly. "Dax loves you. You need to let him know you're not angry with him. Everything else will work itself out."

Kenzi jumped to her feet. "I'm going to call him. Right now."

As she walked out of the room with her phone she heard Asher ask, "Does this mean the game is over and I won?"

His question was quickly followed by the sound of laughter and tiles being thrown at him.

DAX WAS NURSING his first drink an hour into a party he wished he'd said he wouldn't attend. One of Clay's friends had invited both of them to the opening of her restaurant. The place was loud and wall to wall with London's elite crowd. There was a time when Dax would have used the opportunity to network or hook up with one of the women who came to events such as this to meet men like him. He wasn't interested in either that night. He'd come because Clay had asked him to.

Clay came to stand beside him. "Do you know what's

not going to help you get laid tonight—looking like you want to kill whatever is at the bottom of your glass. Lighten up."

Dax handed his drink to a passing server. "Sorry. I have a lot on my mind lately."

Clay sighed. "No, you have one thing on your mind. One person. What I don't understand is why you don't do something about it."

"This isn't about Kenzi."

Clay winked at a woman across the room then said, "Listen, when you first got all moony over her, I'll admit I found some amusement in it, but now you need to get over her. Look at all the beautiful women here tonight. Half of them would go home with you if you gave them the least bit of encouragement. You want to get Kenzi out of your head? Get one of them in your bed. Works every time."

Dax frowned at his friend. "I've got to go. I have an early morning meeting tomorrow."

Clay shrugged. "Suit yourself. Hey, did I tell you I received an inquiry about the Atlantia. You may sell that thing yet."

"Thanks for keeping feelers out there, but I'm considering keeping it. Forward me the information though. I'll follow up on it." Dax hadn't done much with it since he'd returned to London, but there was no reason to hold onto it. No reason that made sense anyway.

Dax's phone buzzed with an incoming call. He checked it and rocked back on his heels in surprise. "It's Kenzi."

Clay gave Dax a pat on the shoulder. "And the universe

chimes in with its vote. You should see your face. Oh, my God, please make me your best man so I can give a long, painfully embarrassing speech that no one feels they can interrupt."

Dax waved Clay away and stepped out of the restaurant. By the time he made it through the crowd he'd missed the call. He didn't give himself time to think about it, he simply called her back.

"Kenzi?"

"Yes."

"Did something happen? Are you okay?"

"I miss you."

Nothing could have prepared him for the wave of emotion that swept through him at those words. "I miss you, too," he said in a husky voice.

He heard her expel a shaky breath. "I'm not angry with you, Dax. I understand why you haven't called."

"You do?"

"My father told me what he said to you."

Which meant she knew he'd left because he didn't love her. "He shouldn't have—"

She cut him off. "It's okay. Don't feel badly about being honest. Being with you taught me that honesty can hurt, but it's the only way to heal. So, I need to be honest with you, Dax. I love you. There has never been anyone in my life who has made me feel as good about myself as you have. You're a good friend, an amazing lover, and I don't care if you can't ever say you love me. The way you listen to me, the way you care about what I care about, is more loving than any man

I've ever known."

Dax paced back and forth on the sidewalk in front of the restaurant. He wanted to tell Kenzi he loved her, he wanted to so badly he felt sick when he couldn't. She deserved so much better than he was giving her. "I've been a miserable bastard without you."

"Then come here. Or I'll go there."

Dax was angry with himself, angry with a past that held him back. A man walked in front of Dax then skittered out of his way after looking at the expression on his face. "You want marriage, kids, the whole happily ever after. I'm not that man, Kenzi. My father went through marriages like some people go through cars. As soon as it wasn't shiny and new he traded it in for a new one. What if I am just like him?"

"Then don't marry me," Kenzi said in a soft tone that took his breath away.

"You don't mean that, Kenzi. You want what your parents have, and if I couldn't give that to you, you'd end up hating me."

"Don't tell me how I will or won't feel. I can't see into the future, so I don't know who I'll be five or ten years from now. Maybe I will feel differently about marriage and children then. All I care about is how I feel today. I don't regret one moment I spent with you. Not one. Do you remember the note you wrote with the music you gave me? You told me that I was stronger than whatever I was facing. You were right. I am strong. I didn't fall apart when you didn't call. I've been working on me and getting myself into a better place. If we don't work out, it'll hurt, Dax. It'll hurt like hell. But I'll survive. I know that now, and you're part of the reason I do. So don't tell me I'll hate you, because that is one thing I know will never happen."

Dax waved to his driver who was watching him from where his car was parked across the street. "If I fly out now I can be at your place before morning."

"I'll wait up."

"No, you should rest. I'll have a six-hour flight to think about nothing but you and all the ways I can show you how much I've missed you."

Kenzi laughed the way she did when she was turned on. He'd never heard a sweeter sound. "I'll try to sleep, but I have a feeling I'll be awake imagining all the same things."

Dax's car pulled up, and he told Kenzi he'd text her when he landed. He knew he had a big, stupid grin on his face, but he didn't care. Kenzi loved him and for the first time the idea didn't terrify him.

Clay came out of the restaurant just as Dax was stepping into his car. "Is everything okay?"

Dax nodded. "I'm flying back to Boston tonight. I don't know when I'll be back."

Clay smiled and saluted him. "I'll start working on my speech."

Dax didn't correct his assumption. He could explain everything to him later. All that mattered right then was getting on a plane and getting back to Kenzi.

Chapter Eighteen

WAITING FOR DAX to arrive was torture, but it was followed by indescribable pleasure when he finally walked through Kenzi's door. She threw herself in his arms and kissed him with every bit of love she'd been holding back.

There was no time for talking; that would come later. Kenzi tore at his clothes while he tore at hers. His mouth claimed hers deeply, completely. They'd barely closed the door before they were mostly naked and Kenzi was straddling Dax's waist, her back against the wall while he kissed her feverishly.

Every touch felt better than the last as Kenzi gave herself over to the passion. She dug her hands into his hair and kissed him wildly as his hands removed the last of their clothing.

His mouth moved to her neck then her breasts. He held her easily against him and kissed his way down the valley between them. He was taking his time, teasing her, making sure she was ready for him, but Kenzi didn't want to go slowly. She wanted him inside her—now.

He paused to sheathe his cock and murmured how much he missed her. She whispered something back, but she was beyond caring about words. His cock nudged at her sex for entry, and she begged Dax to take her then.

He lost all control at that and pounded upward into her. Kenzi used what leverage she could to move up and down with him then gave herself over to the power of his claiming. With Dax there was no shame, no fear that he would hurt her. There was only the joy of his body intimately joining with hers. She trusted him completely, and that freed her to enjoy him in a way she'd never found with another man.

She came a few seconds before he did and they stayed still against the wall, still connected, trying to catch their breath.

"Fuck, Kenzi, I meant to go slowly."

Kenzi clenched her inner muscles around him and cupped his face with her hands. "Are you kidding? That was perfect."

"You're perfect." He smiled and kissed her. It was a different sort of kiss, an I've-missed-your-friendship caress that was just as powerful as the earlier kisses but in an entirely different way. Passion, Kenzi knew, couldn't be relied on to stay, but this—this would endure.

He put her down gently and cleaned himself off then picked her up and carried her to her bed.

The second time they made love brought Kenzi to tears. Dax was so gentle, so concerned with her pleasure, she knew she'd made the right choice to take him as he was. She was more than ready when she straddled his thick, hard cock. She eased herself down onto him, taking him deeply inside her then began to move her hips up and down. She had loved it earlier when he'd taken her against the wall, and she loved how he now gave her control. She whispered orders to him. "Kiss my neck. Lick me here." All the while she kept a steady rhythm that brought her body closer and closer to another climax. It was a slow pleasure, an enjoyment of how their bodies connected. Dax sat up and moved with her, matching her rhythm. When they finally did come, she was wrapped around Dax with her feet behind him, and it was a total, full-body experience that left him shaken while she clung to him. He adjusted their position so he could drop onto his back, and Kenzi collapsed on him.

Kenzi joked, "I may never be able to move again."

"You? Remember I'm older than you."

Kenzi kissed his chest. "I have no complaints."

"Thank God," he said and kissed her on the lips gently.

They lay there, holding each other for a long time. Eventually, Kenzi asked, "Did you even bring any luggage?"

"No, I went straight from the restaurant to my plane. I'll have someone drop off some clothes later. They're getting used to bringing my things here."

Kenzi was tempted to say he could bring as much stuff as he wanted, but she didn't want him to think she was pressuring him. Dax was in her life again. As her mother had said, everything else would sort itself out.

Kenzi ran her hand along the strong muscles of his neck. "I know that you offered to help Dean."

He stopped her hand with his and brought it to his

mouth for a kiss. "I didn't do it to get you back into my bed, Kenzi."

"Technically, this is my bed, but I know that, Dax. You did it because of what Dean did for me."

"Yes. I knew you felt that you owed him something, and I felt as if I did, too."

Tears filled Kenzi's eyes. "That is the most beautiful thing anyone has ever said to me."

Dax looked uncomfortable with her praise, but then he smiled. "If you stick with me, Kenzi, you will come across many people who see me the way your family does. I never cared what anyone thought of me until you."

"My family encouraged me to call you. They'll come around."

Dax hugged Kenzi to his chest. "I don't care if they do as long as I never give you a reason to look at me the way they did."

Kenzi snuggled against Dax. Her heart was overflowing with love for him. She tempered it, though. She remembered feeling that if people knew the real her they wouldn't love her. Was that how Dax felt? If so, he had a lot to learn about love, and she wanted to be the one to teach him.

DAX HELD KENZI through the night. While she dozed he spent hours thinking about the differences between them, but also how they were the same. Kenzi refused to give up on him. She'd chosen her course and was sticking to it even if he couldn't say the words she wanted to hear.

In some ways, Kenzi was stronger than he was. It wasn't

something he would acknowledge out loud, but he knew it in his heart. She had faced her fears and won, and she hadn't let that battle rob her of who she was.

Dax thought about who he might have been if his father had lived, or if he'd ever known his mother. Life had challenged him again and again, and he had sold his soul to stay on top.

Kenzi hadn't. Somehow she'd remained a good person.

He kissed her forehead as she slept. He was at a crossroads, and he knew it. If he walked away from Kenzi again, he knew who he would be for the rest of his life. What he didn't know, though, was who he would be if he stayed.

He whispered, "I want to love you, Kenzi. Show me how." Kenzi moved against him as if she'd heard him, but she didn't wake.

Taffy padded into the room and whined to be let up on the bed. Dax dropped a pillow beside the bed and said, "You can stay in here, but you're not coming on the bed." Taffy whined again, and Dax petted her head while she settled onto the pillow. He glanced down at her, and she gave him eyes that were so pitiful he laughed. "That doesn't work with me. Dogs belong outside, you're lucky to be in here at all."

Taffy moved her head lovingly against his hand, and he felt the rough skin that circled her neck. He thought about what she must have gone through and how much joy she brought Kenzi and kept petting her head absently. "You're a good dog, Taffy."

Taffy whined softly.

"But you're still not sleeping on this bed."

Dax fell asleep with Kenzi cuddled to one side of him while his hand hung off the side of the bed to calm Taffy. When he woke he found Kenzi watching him. She was up on one elbow, her beautiful breasts bared to him. As soon as she saw he was awake she smiled, and he caught his breath at how something so simple could render him speechless.

She kissed him and chuckled. "If you let her in the bed, we'll never get her out."

Dax looked over and realized why his other side felt warm. Taffy was tucked into the crook of his arm as if he'd put her there. He frowned at her. Her response was to wag her tail and snuggle closer to him. "I told her to stay on the floor."

Kenzi laughed. "Uh huh."

Dax smiled. "I did. I've made grown men cry just by showing up at a meeting, why can't I keep this dog off the bed?"

Kenzi gave him a sweet kiss. "Because she adores you, just like I do. I'm glad you came back, Dax."

Dax ran a hand up and down Kenzi's bare back. "You can say how you feel, Kenzi. I won't leave again. I belong here, Kenzi. I've never felt so sure about anything. I don't know how to do this—a relationship. Do I stay here? Do you stay with me? I don't know what we call it—"

"Then I love you, Dax." Kenzi silenced him with another kiss then said, "I don't care what you call what we have. I don't care where we stay. There are no rules to this, Dax, except that we're honest with each other no matter what. If we do that, everything else will work out. You taught me that."

I can do that.

Over the next month, Dax took Kenzi's words to heart and let himself enjoy simply being with her. They went for jogs together, took Taffy for walks, went to the movies with Lexi and Willa. Dax watched Kenzi's confidence blossom, and he liked to think he had played a part in her transformation.

He was sitting in his office one day, smiling for no reason, when Clay called and asked him when he was returning to London.

"No time soon."

"Does that mean you're not sick of Kenzi yet?"

"Every day I'm with her makes me want to be with her another day."

Clay didn't make a joke. They both knew Dax meant it.

"So, you're moving your headquarters to Boston?"

"Kenzi says she'll continent hop with me. Once things settle down we'll probably spend half of our time in London and half of our time here."

"I didn't think it would last, Dax, but you sound happy."

"I am." He realized something then that he'd known but denied for a while. "I love her, Clay."

"Rewind there, buddy. What did you just say?"

Dax looked out of the Boston skyline and in a louder voice, said, "I love her. I love waking up to her. I love coming home to her. I love the way she knows what I'm thinking when I'm still trying to figure it out."

"That's a lot of love. Have you told her?"

Dax shook his head even though Clay couldn't see him. "It's not something you just blurt out."

"Oh, I think it is. That's probably the most common way it gets said. That and in the backseats of cars in high school, but I digress. If you make a big deal out of it, you might as well hire a skywriter."

Dax looked up at the clouds. "No. That would be tacky. Right?"

Clay laughed. "If I weren't such a good friend I would completely take advantage of how lost you are right now. Just tell her how you feel."

"You tell everyone you love them. You probably say it to Kate when she brings you coffee. I've never said it."

"I don't love Kate."

"That was an example."

"I'm just saying, I talk to Kate, but there's nothing there."

Dax glanced back at the door of his office. "Is there something going on between you and my secretary?" That would explain why Clay had been around as much as he had. "Seriously, don't sleep with her. She's good. I don't want to lose her."

"I'm not sleeping with her."

"Whatever." Dax wasn't sure if he believed him, but he had more important things on his mind. "I'll talk to you later."

Dax paged his secretary to come into his office. As soon as she stepped inside he said, "Kate, I love Kenzi."

Kate looked at him cautiously. "I guessed as much."

"Get a notepad and come back. We need to brainstorm how I should tell her."

A huge smile spread across Kate's face. "Are you kidding? Who needs to brainstorm that?" When he didn't say anything she forced a more serious expression on her face. "Of course I'll help you." She darted to her desk and returned with notepad and pen. She was also smart enough to take the task seriously.

Dax started pacing the room. "I want it to be special. Romantic, but not over the top. I want to show Kenzi how important she is to me, not just say the words."

Kate made a face. "Perhaps something with her family?"

Chapter Nineteen

"I DON'T THINK that's a good idea," Kenzi said to Dax as they sat in a circular booth at their favorite Boston restaurant.

"It's time, Kenzi," Dax said.

"You and I hosting game night for my family? No. We're happy. I don't want to do anything that could change that."

"Change can be good." Dax held Kenzi's hand in one of his and looked into her eyes. "You can't keep me away from your family forever."

Yes, I can. "Not forever, just for a while longer."

"You're taking me to your brother's wedding. Wouldn't it be best if I spent some time with them before then?"

Memories of the one time Dax had been to her parents' house came back far too easily for Kenzi to agree. "I'm nervous about the wedding, but at least I know they'll all be on their best behavior that day." Kenzi nervously arranged and rearranged the silverware beside her plate. "Can we agree to do something with them after the wedding?"

Dax frowned. "Is it me or them you don't trust?"

Kenzi felt awful. Dax looked genuinely upset by her refusal. "I trust you, Dax. It's just that my family knows we're together now. They've come around to the idea, but you know my brothers. I mean, you've met them. Do I really have to say more than that?"

Dax leaned over and kissed her cheek. "You know there's nothing they could say that would change what we have."

"I know." Kenzi said the words even though she wasn't certain she meant them. Dax didn't look satisfied with her answer, but he didn't push her.

He looked like he wanted to say more, but he didn't. Kenzi felt badly that she'd blocked his idea, but she saw too many ways it could go wrong.

She and Dax were good together. He got along with her friends. She got along with his. They'd traveled together, practically moved into each other's places, and every day had been as good if not better than the day before. She wouldn't risk losing that.

Dax worked during the day and now so did Kenzi. Mornings were rushed, but they made time for each other. Most evenings involved walking Taffy and catching up with what each had done that day. Dax fit into her life perfectly; Kenzi just wasn't as confident that he fit into her family. Neither had asked her to choose one over the other, and that was something she was grateful for.

She and Dax didn't have issues, so why introduce any? Her family would want to know the answers to all the questions Kenzi wasn't asking. She couldn't risk them pushing him away again.

She gave Dax a sad look. "I'm sorry, Dax, no. I don't

want to host game night for my family."

Dax didn't argue with her, but she could tell he wasn't happy with her answer. She wasn't thrilled with it either, but she didn't feel like she had much choice. She wanted to say, *I'm doing this for us, Dax,* but she felt she'd already said too much.

THE NEXT DAY, Dax sat in his car outside the Barrington family home. He'd driven himself there and had spent the last few minutes drumming his fingers on the steering wheel.

When he and Kate had designed the perfect way for him to tell Kenzi that he loved her, it had sounded simple. He would invite her family over to show her he was ready to take their relationship to the next step. While waiting for her family to arrive he would walk up behind her, pull her back into his arms, and whisper in her ear that he loved her. His first version of the night had involved just him and Kenzi and a whole lot of intimate celebrating, but Kate's idea held some merit. Kenzi's family was important to her and what better way to show her how much he loved her than giving them another chance to string him up by his testicles?

He shook his head to clear that idea. A month had gone by without word from them. If they'd wanted to block Kenzi from seeing him, they'd had plenty of opportunity to do so before then. He had to believe they had at least agreed to tolerate his presence in her life.

It was time to move that relationship along as well.

Dax had left a message for each of Kenzi's brothers, except Andrew who was still out of the country. He'd asked them to meet him at their parents' house.

Dax stepped out of his car. The door of the house opened, and Sophie waved to him. It was impossible not to return her smile. *That's one on my side.*

Dale stood just behind her and nodded his welcome. *That's two.*

He gave Sophie a kiss to her cheek for a greeting and shook Dale's hand.

"Everyone is inside. You definitely piqued their curiosity with your call." Dale gave Dax a fatherly pat on the arm. "I hope you know what you're doing."

"I do, sir."

"Dax, call me Dale."

Dax nodded and followed Sophie and Dale into their living room where their sons and Emily were gathered. Asher impressed him by crossing the room to shake his hand. That act released some of the tension, and each of the other brothers greeted him in much the same way. Emily gave him a quick hug and a covert thumbs-up that brought a smile to his face.

Dale said, "You asked us all to be here so you could say something. What is it, son?"

Dax hesitated. In all his years in business, he'd spoken before many different groups of people from all walks of life. He'd never let any of them intimidate him, but to speak to this group he had to gather his courage. It wasn't that he was afraid of what they'd say to him, but rather he didn't want to disappoint Kenzi by not saying the right things to them. "I'm here to ask your permission to marry Kenzi."

Sophie gasped and brought a hand to her mouth.

Emily hugged Asher's arm to her.

Dale clarified with the question, "Mine?"

Dax shook his head and waved a hand in a gesture that meant all of them. "Yours. All of you. I know how important Kenzi is to you and how important you are to her. What you don't know is how important she is to me. I love her more than I ever thought I could love anyone. I intend to ask her to marry me, and if she says yes, I will spend the rest of my life showing her how grateful I am to have found her. I haven't lived a perfect life. I can't go back in time and change what I've done. All I can do is tell you that I am a better man because Kenzi is in my life. Before I propose, I want to make sure you'll all be happy for us. Kenzi would be devastated if you weren't. So, give me your blessing or tell me what I need to do to make it so you can support this, because I will be joining this family."

There was a long pause when Dax finished. He expected Dale to be the one to speak, but to his surprise it was Sophie. She looked at each of her sons in turn then said, "Dax is brutally honest, but our family could use a dose of that. If you have a problem with him say it now. Because I, for one, would love to be planning two weddings this year."

Dale put his arm around Sophie's waist. "Me, too. It took courage to come here and say what Dax did. If you can't put aside your issues with him, be brave enough to say it now, and we'll work through it. I won't have a repeat of his last visit. That's not who we are."

Dax braced himself for what either Ian or Asher would

say. He didn't expect that it would be easy to win them over, but this was something he wanted to do for Kenzi. Something he would do, no matter how difficult they made it at first.

Emily gave Asher a long look, then she let go of his arm and nudged him toward Dax. Asher nodded to Ian.

Ian rubbed his jaw thoughtfully and said, "We have all done things we regret. Asher more than most."

Asher narrowed his eyes at him. "See what happens when you let a politician speak for you. What he means is that we can put the past behind us if you can."

Grant added dryly, "Which is as close to an apology as you'll get from Asher. I'd take it, Dax."

Lance cocked his head to one side. "Really? See, I'd totally take advantage of the situation. Dax, Emily is right there watching him. What could he do?"

Sophie chimed in, "Boys, be serious. Barringtons marry for life. I don't want to be breaking up brawls between you in front of my grandchildren. Are we good?"

Asher shook Dax's hand again. "We're good, as long as you're good to Kenzi."

Dax said, "Understood."

Ian shook his hand, followed by Lance and Grant. Dale gave him a brief hug, as did Emily. Sophie hugged him longer, but he wasn't about to complain. There was a time when Sophie's affection would have made him uncomfortable; now it was comforting. The meeting had worked out better than any scenario he'd imagined.

He thought he was in the clear until Emily asked, "So,

have you planned your proposal? Asher asked me in front of everyone at an auction." Her eyes shone with emotion, and Asher kissed her on the top of her head. "He donated half a town in the name of my museum as a place where all kinds of artists could learn their craft."

The look Asher shot him was an amused, *Beat that.* Shit.

Then an idea came to him, one that built off what Lance had said earlier about taking advantage of the opportunities at hand. He'd never been one to pass one up. He turned his most charming smile on Sophie. "Would you help me plan the perfect proposal? Imagine how happy Kenzi would be if she knew you were part of it somehow." Dax shot a smug smile at Asher. "All of you."

Sophie was beaming. "We would love that. You could do it here. And you're right, if she knew we all helped to plan it, she'd know we accept you. That would mean more to her than anything else."

Asher narrowed his eyes at Dax, but in a similar fashion to how he'd looked at Ian. Dax took it as a sign that he could indeed become one of them. Until then Dax would have said he had no desire to be part of a family, outside of the one he would build with Kenzi. As he tossed around ideas with Kenzi's parents and brothers, he couldn't deny that he wanted to belong there with them. He respected Dale, and Sophie was loving in a way he'd once yearned for his own mother to be. Kenzi's brothers were—well, he was far from perfect himself.

Chapter Twenty

KENZI HATED LEAVING Dax behind, but she told herself there was no other option. When her mother had called and told her they were gathering for a game night, something that had been unofficially suspended since Dax had returned, Kenzi hadn't wanted to say no. She had spent every night with Dax, so although she'd seen her parents, she hadn't seen some of her brothers in over a month.

Kenzi felt even worse because Dax had asked about hosting a game night together, and she had refused him. *Now here I am heading off to one without him.*

She didn't want Dax to feel excluded, but she also remembered the first time she'd taken him home all too well. She loved her family, and she loved Dax. She wasn't willing to cut either out of her life, nor was she ready to risk losing Dax again.

Dax wants to try again with my family. Doesn't he deserve the chance to?

Kenzi pulled into her parents' driveway and sat in her car thinking. *This is wrong. Dax wouldn't do this to me.* She took out her phone and called Dax.

"Kenzi?"

"Dax, I feel like an ass. I should have brought you with me tonight. I'm so sorry I didn't. I—"

"Kenzi, it's okay."

"No, it's not. You would never leave me home. I can't do that to you. We'll come on another night together. We'll figure this out together, Dax."

Dax was quiet for a moment, and Kenzi almost burst into tears. "Go see your family, Kenzi. I want you to. I'm working on something I've already put off too long. Go. Enjoy tonight. I'll see you later."

He didn't sound upset. "Are you sure?"

"I'm sure. Kenzi, I know you've missed them. I'm happy you're there tonight."

Kenzi felt better and worse all at the same time. She would have said she loved him just then, but she held it back because he already knew how she felt. He never pressured her; she vowed to never pressure him. "I won't be late."

"I may be."

"Okay. Bye, Dax."

After they hung up Kenzi squared her shoulders and headed into her parents' home. She kissed her father in greeting. When he asked her how she was, she answered honestly, "Miserable."

Dale looked concerned. "What happened?"

Sophie came up beside her husband. "Kenzi? Are you upset?"

Kenzi wiped away a tear. "I told myself I could come here without Dax and enjoy myself. He told me he was okay with it, but now that I'm here I realize that I can't be. I love him so much. Mom, you would never go anywhere Dad wasn't welcome, would you?"

Sophie shook her head. "I wouldn't."

Kenzi wiped away another tear. "Dad, I know Dax isn't perfect, but he's perfect for me."

Dale looked at Sophie; she shook her head. He put his arm around Kenzi and guided her inside. "It'll all work out. Have a little faith, Kenzi."

Sophie flanked her other side as they walked into the house. "Your father is right. You're already here. Don't leave. You might be surprised how much you enjoy yourself."

Kenzi wanted to agree, but she'd vowed not to lie to her parents again. When she walked into the living room and saw her brothers there, laughing and joking, she wanted to smack every one of them.

Emily came over and hugged her. She searched her face then asked, "Are you okay, Kenzi?"

Kenzi took a deep breath and then turned to her brothers. "No, I am not. I left Dax behind because, although I have just had the best month of my life with him, I'm so scared that if I bring him here one of you will go after him again. I know you think you're protecting me, but you'll end up driving me away. I love you, and I've even really started to enjoy these game nights, but I won't come to another without Dax. If you want me in your life, you'll have to make room for him, too, because he's part of mine." When she finished she took several gulps of air and waited for her brothers' responses.

Lance made a face at Grant. "Well, that answers the question of if she knows."

Kenzi pounced on his comment. "Knows what?"

Grant gave Lance a hearty smack to the back and spoke for him. "We talked and decided Dax isn't as bad as we thought."

Kenzi looked at Asher. "Is that true?"

"Are you really happy with him, Kenzi?" Asher asked.

"I really am."

"Then he's welcomed here."

Kenzi turned to Ian. "Do you feel the same way?"

Ian crossed over and gave Kenzi a hug. "We want you to be happy, Kenzi. That's all we ever wanted."

It felt too easy. Kenzi studied each of her brothers' expressions. They looked like they were hiding something. "When did you have this talk?"

Sophie came over and took Kenzi's arm. "Emily had a fabulous idea for a scavenger hunt we could do right here. She put strings to four things in the house. We follow the string, find the clue, come back, report it to our group, and try to solve the puzzle. It sounds fun. She put a lot of planning into to this, Kenzi. We have to at least try it."

"I don't really understand," Kenzi said. "What's the game?"

Emily pointed to a string on the floor. "Let's just play it, and you'll figure it out. Follow the string to a clue. Come back and tell us what it is."

Shaking her head, Kenzi gave in and followed a string out of the room, down the hall, and to the kitchen. There on the counter was a stuffed animal, a white sheep with a small baby lamb attached. She brought it back to the living room. "Sheep? I don't get it."

Lance rolled his eyes. "I'll get the second clue." He came back a moment later with a paper and put it beside the stuffed animal. "It's a will."

Dale said, "Ian, why don't you find the next?"

Ian headed off into another room then returned with a mirror. He placed it beside the other two items.

Emily took Asher by the hand. "The last one is ours. Come on." They followed a string into the hall then came back with a painting of the Virgin Mary. They placed it on the table beside the three other items.

Grant rubbed his chin. "What could these items mean?"

Lance said, "What do you think, Kenzi? Can you solve it?"

The way her family was watching her made Kenzi wonder if they were losing their minds. Had too many game nights driven them to this? She was tempted to tell them that she'd said what she had to say and really wasn't in the mood for a game, but there was something different about this game. It felt important, but Kenzi couldn't figure out why. She looked at the items on the table and said, "Sheep. Mirror. Painting. Document." She shrugged. Sophie urged her to try again using different words. Kenzi took a second look at the items. "Mary. Lamb. Will. Reflection. I've got nothing."

Dax stepped into the room, and Kenzi gasped in surprised. She rushed to his side. "Dax, you came." She turned to her brothers to gauge their reaction.

Dax kissed her gently on the cheek and said, "I told you I had something I had to do tonight. Something I've put off too long. This was it."

"This?"

Dax led her to the table, and he rearranged the items. "Will. Ewe. Mary. Me." Then he dropped to one knee, took out a small box, and held it out to her. "I love you, Kenzi. I've loved you since the night you threw up on my shoe, but I tried to deny it. You scared me that night, and I've been a wreck since then. Say yes, Kenzi."

Kenzi looked from Dax to the faces of her family. "You planned this? All of you?"

Sophie said, "It was Dax's idea, but your brothers helped him plan it."

In a voice thick with emotion, Asher said, "No one should have to choose between the person they love and their family. I know I couldn't." He wrapped his arms around Emily, who was beaming.

Dax waved the ring. "You can say yes anytime, Kenzi."

Kenzi burst into laughter. "Yes. Yes. Of course, yes, Dax."

Dax slipped the ring on her finger then stood and pulled her into his arms for a deep kiss. Nothing in Kenzi's life had prepared her for how happy she was in that moment.

She hugged Dax, walked around and hugged each member of her family, then went back to hugging Dax. As her head cleared she remembered how she'd felt when she first arrived, and she gave Dax a playful swat. "I can't believe you didn't tell me."

He kissed the tip of her nose. "I almost did."

She looked at her brothers. "And you. You let me go on and on about Dax when you knew he was here." She glanced up at Dax. "Did you hear all that?"

"Every word," Dax said and his expression turned serious. "No one has ever defended me the way you did. I don't have a lot of experience with love, but something tells me I've chosen the best teacher."

Kenzi went on her tiptoes and kissed him on the mouth. "Oh, I'll teach you." Ideas of how were already bringing an excited flush to her face.

There was a general groan and Dale suggested they save *that* conversation for later.

"How about some coffee and cake?" Sophie asked.

A SHORT TIME later, Dax sat with his untouched coffee and watched Kenzi on the phone with her friends. A huge smile spread across his face as he imagined their lives together. There was always a moment after every business deal when the final signature hit the paperwork and it became real— when there was no turning back or walking away. Dax had always found power in that moment. When he chose a path he stuck to it regardless of the obstacles he encountered. He'd never been a man who gave up once he set his course.

It was that sense of commitment Dax felt the moment Kenzi said yes to him. He was in this for the long haul.

I am not my father.

He wasn't with Kenzi because he wanted to show her off

to his friends. Her value wasn't one that would decline as they aged. He was with her because he never wanted to go back to the man he'd been before her.

Before Kenzi, he'd thought he had everything because his life was full of what many people considered signs of success, but he couldn't remember ever feeling as good as he felt whenever he was with her.

Even being with her family felt—right.

He looked around the room. Sophie was smiling at something her sons were joking about. Dale was looking on with a look of love on his face that once would have confused Dax. He understood now. Suddenly Dale's decision to give up his career made sense. Everything that mattered was right there in that room.

Asher leaned over and asked, "Do you still have a security detail following Kenzi?"

Dax nodded.

"She won't be happy when she finds that out," he said even though he looked as though he approved.

Dax shrugged. "I'm willing to deal with that conversation as long as she's safe."

Asher folded his arms across his chest. "When you have a little sister, you want to protect her. No one could be good enough, but you're not as bad as I thought."

Dax's smile widened. "You live up to your reputation as an arrogant bastard and your brothers are just as bad, but that's how I know I belong here. Can you imagine me with the perfect family? I'd scare the shit out of them."

Asher threw his head back and laughed. "That you

would."

Pausing as she walked behind them, Emily dipped her head down next to Asher's. "I like seeing you two getting along."

Asher kissed Emily's cheek. "He's growing on me."

Kenzi wrapped her arms around Dax's neck from behind and flashed her diamond before all four of them. "You'd better hurry up and get married so we can see if a family wedding is survivable, or if there is an elopement in our future."

Dax said, "I'll marry you any day you choose, anywhere. I don't care what it looks like as long as it ends with you coming home with me."

Kenzi and Emily sighed audibly.

Emily said, "Asher, isn't that romantic?"

Asher grudgingly agreed, and the women laughed.

Kenzi hugged him so tightly it almost choked him, but Dax didn't complain. He loved seeing her like this. Happy. Free. She said, "I'd love a beach wedding on an island. Maybe the one where we met?"

Asher's face suddenly turned serious. "Mom won't go to the Bahamas."

Dax glanced back at Kenzi, and she said softly, "My parents were on an island when Kent and I were born. She hasn't gone to one since."

Dax took her hands in his. He remembered how Kenzi dreamed of everyone being together and happy. He couldn't bring her brother back for her, but he thought of a location that might work for both Kenzi and her mother. "Clay owns several hotels in Clearwater, Florida. Some are right on the beach. Clearwater is not quite an island. It's all connected by roads and bridges, but Clay says the sand is white and can't be beat for beauty."

Kenzi hugged him so tightly she nearly choked him again. "I love that idea. And you're right, it doesn't matter where the wedding is as long as it ends with us together."

Dax didn't have the words to express the love that surged through him just then, so he turned and kissed her. It lasted longer than he meant it to.

Dale cleared his throat loudly across the table. "Kenzi. Dax. We'll see you two tomorrow."

Kenzi broke off the kiss with a laugh. "I believe they're throwing us out."

Dax stood still holding Kenzi's hand in his. "I believe they are." He nodded at her father. "See you tomorrow, Dale."

"Dad. Call me Dad," Dale said and stood.

That simple request touched Dax deeply. He wasn't the type to show his emotions outwardly, but his voice was husky when he said, "Dad."

Kenzi looked from her father back to Dax with huge round eyes.

Looking into the eyes of the woman he loved reminded him of why he wouldn't see her family the next day. He leaned over the table to shake Dale's hand. "I'm taking Kenzi out of the country tonight for part two of her surprise."

Kenzi's mouth dropped open. "You mean there is more?"

It was time to see if Kate actually did deserve that raise.

"I'm taking you to a business meeting."

"Me?"

"Yes, I need to decide what to do with a certain island resort I own. The family I bought it from couldn't afford to maintain it, but it had been in their family for generations. I'm meeting with them to see if we can come to an agreement that would involve them taking over the day-to-day running of it in exchange for partial ownership of it. They think I'm joking, but once they meet you they'll understand. I don't want to sell the place we met, but I don't want to build our future on a memory of who I was. I can't go back and undo everything I've done, but I can undo this one. And with your help, Kenzi, I can do it right this time."

Kenzi looked up at Dax with such love in her eyes that Dax knew he finally had what he'd never allowed himself to admit he wanted—a home. His life with Kenzi would probably be filled with children and pets. It would be messy and complicated, but it would be full of love.

And he couldn't imagine wanting it any other way.

Chapter Twenty-One

TWO WEEKS LATER Kenzi was attending the opening of Emily's Tactile Museum of Art with Dax. It was a large event, but only a hint of what would be thrown for the opening of the education complex her brother was building for Emily in New Hampshire.

Kenzi and Dax were both dressed to the nines, but the one who'd received the most attention as they'd entered the event had been Taffy. Her hair had grown in well and her scars were finally covered, but the journey she'd been through was forever immortalized in an exhibit at the museum. People of all ages came over to say how beautiful Taffy was and how deeply her story had touched them.

Kenzi and Dax were working their way through the crowd when a man approached them and handed Kenzi his card. He was a producer and said he was interested in making Taffy's story into a movie. Kenzi met Dax's eyes briefly, curious to see his reaction.

Dax asked what she thought he would: "Is that what you want, Kenzi?"

Kenzi looked at the healthy dog who was happily tucked

beneath Dax's arm. Kenzi leaned lovingly against Dax. "No, I already have I want." She leaned over and gave Taffy a scratch beneath her chin. "And so does Taffy."

Dax bent to kiss her briefly, and the man walked away. The moment was broken by Lance appearing beside them. "Kenzi, is Willa coming tonight?"

Kenzi looked at Dax and hid a smile. They'd spoken about how Lance had a sweet spot for Willa. "She said she might. Should I tell her you're looking for her?"

Her brother went a light shade of pink. "No. I was just curious." He waved a hand around dismissively. "Hey, I have a question for you."

Completely at a loss, Kenzi shrugged one shoulder. "Okay."

"Emily asked me about Mom's sister, Patrice. She's really curious about her. She said she's reading her journal and found notes about you and Kent along with a string of numbers and an address. She said it was odd. Emily wants to ask Mom about it. I told her *hell no*, but I wanted to see what you thought."

Kenzi gripped Dax's arm. "Mom handled everything with me so well, but she still won't talk about Kent. I don't think it's a good idea to ask her anything about her sister. Do you agree, Dax?"

Dax leaned in. "I wouldn't read anyone's journal, but if I did and I found something in it that didn't sound right, I'd have to ask about it."

Kenzi looked back at Lance. "What does Asher think?"

Lance rolled his eyes skyward "He doesn't want to know

about it. He says the past is the past."

"But you think there might be something to this?" Kenzi bit her bottom lip. "Aunt Patrice wasn't a happy woman. I can't imagine what she'd write about."

Lance asked, "So, you'll read it?"

"Only if you do," Kenzi said then turned to Dax. Lance did, too.

Dax shook his head. "No. Keep me out of this." Kenzi gave him hopeful eyes.

Lance said, "We need someone who can be objective."

Dax groaned. "I'll read it once, but you two will owe me. What are you so afraid of, anyway? What could possibly be in some dead, old woman's journal?"

The End

Be the first to hear about my releases

ruthcardello.com/signup

One random newsletter subscriber will be chosen every month in 2015. The chosen subscriber will receive a $100 eGift Card! Sign up today by clicking on the link above!

Acknowledgements

I am so grateful to everyone who was part of the process of creating *Always Mine*. Thank you to:

Nicole Sanders at Trevino Creative Graphic Design for my new cover. You are amazing!

My very patient beta readers. You know who you are. Thank you for kicking my butt when I need it.

My editors: Karen Lawson, Janet Hitchcock, and Marion Archer.

My Roadies for making me smile each day when I log on my computer. So many of you have become friends. Was there life before the Roadies? I'm sure there was, but it wasn't have as much fun.

Thank you to my husband, Tony, who is a saint—simple as that.

Other Books by Ruth

The Legacy Collection:

Also available in audiobook format

Where my billionaires began.

Book 1: Maid for the Billionaire (available at all major eBook stores for FREE!)

Book 2: For Love or Legacy

Book 3: Bedding the Billionaire

Book 4: Saving The Sheikh

Book 5: Rise of the Billionaire

Book 6: Breaching the Billionaire: Alethea's Redemption

Book 7: A Corisi Christmas Novella

The Andrades

Also available in audiobook format

A spin off series of the Legacy Collection with cameos from characters you love from that series.

Recipe For Love, An Andrade Christmas Novella

Book 1: Come Away With Me (available at all major eBook stores for FREE!)

Book 2: Home to Me

Book 3: Maximum Risk

Book 4: Somewhere Along the Way

Book 5: Loving Gigi

The Barringtons

A new, seven book series about the Andrade's Boston cousins.

The first series in the Barrington Billionaire WORLD.

Book 1: Always Mine

Book 2: Stolen Kisses (Available for pre-order now)

Book 3: Trade It All (Coming 2016)

Book 4: Let It Burn (Coming 2016)

Book 5: More Than Love (Coming 2017)

Book 6: Forever Now (Coming 2017)

Book 7: Never Goodbye (Coming 2017)

*Look for a linked series set in the same world, written by Jeannette Winters (my sister).

You won't have to read her series to enjoy mine, but it sure will make it more fun. Characters will appear in both series.

Author Jeannette Winters

Book 1: One White Lie

Book 2: Table For Two (Coming in April)

Book 3: You and Me Make Three (Coming 2016)

Book 4: Virgin for the Fourth Time (Coming 2016)

Book 5: His for Five Nights (Coming 2017)

Book 6: After Six (Coming 2017)

Lone Star Burn Series:

Hot, fun romances that roam from the country to the city and back.

Book 1: Taken, Not Spurred

Book 2: Tycoon Takedown

Book 3: Taken Home

Book 4: (coming October, 2016)

The Temptation Series:

Guaranteed to put you on Santa's naughty list.

Book 1: Twelve Days of Temptation

Book 2: Be My Temptation

Two hot novellas about one sizzling couple.

Other Books:

Taken By a Trillionaire

Ruth Cardello, JS Scott, Melody Anne.

Three hot fantasies about alpha princes and the women who tame them.

Author Jeannette Winters

The Billionaire's Secret: Betting On You Series: Book One

The Billionaire's Masquerade: Betting On You Series: Book Two

The Billionaire's Longshot: Betting on You Series: Book Three

The Billionaire's Jackpot: Betting on You Series: Book Four

All Bets Off: Betting On You Series: Book Five

Author Biography

Ruth Cardello was born the youngest of 11 children in a small city in northern Rhode Island. She spent her young adult years moving as far away as she could from her large extended family. She lived in Boston, Paris, Orlando, New York—then came full circle and moved back to Rhode Island. She now happily lives one town over from the one she was born in. For her, family trumped the warmer weather and international scene.

She was an educator for 20 years, the last 11 as a kindergarten teacher. When her school district began cutting jobs, Ruth turned a serious eye toward her second love– writing and has never been happier. When she's not writing, you can find her chasing her children around her small farm, riding her horses, or connecting with her readers online.

Contact Ruth:
Website: RuthCardello.com
Email: Minouri@aol.com
FaceBook: Author Ruth Cardello
Twitter: @RuthieCardello

Made in the USA
Coppell, TX
06 February 2020

15404335R20144